The Fu Adventures of Solo

The World's Most Dangerous Dog

By J.R.R. Langley

Illustrations by Stefanie Schultz
Series Editor Katherine Perkins

Austin, TX • London, UK

www.heavy.media

solosstory.com

Table of Contents

1. Solo Plays Golf

Dad loved playing golf. When he wasn't rummaging around in his old workshop, "Mending things that didn't need mending," as his wife put it, he could be found on most weekends walking around the local golf course, pulling his old, but still useful, bag of golf clubs on a battered, old, two-wheeled cart. Whatever the weather, Dad would be out, often with his head bowed against the wind and rain.

Dad was quite happy to play by himself as he often found the solitude relaxing. With a young, boisterous family at home, playing golf was what he called "Dad's quiet time." Away from all the noise at home, Dad could think and mentally recharge his batteries so he could face his work as a lawyer and life at home with the kids. And Solo. He could never, ever forget Solo.

Solo, it seemed, was quite capable of causing havoc even if he didn't mean to. How could Dad forget the time Solo interrupted a tennis match at Wimbledon, or the time he had driven the family car into a pond? It was not surprising, therefore, that Dad viewed golf not so as much a game, but as more of a time for reflection and solitude.

Solo had often seen Dad pack his golf clubs into the back of the family SUV and would wonder what it was that Dad would do for half a day, even in the rain. And what was the purpose of those strange looking sticks? As much as he hinted at Dad that he wanted to come along one day to see what all the fuss was about, he was never invited to do so.

That didn't stop Solo from trying to get invited. Whenever he would spy Dad cleaning his clubs and the back of the SUV open, Solo knew that soon Dad would be leaving to do something interesting with those sticks. And if ever someone was doing something interesting without Solo, Solo would make it his mission to find out exactly what was going on.

And so it was, on a particularly wet and drizzly Saturday morning while the rest of the family was still in bed, that Solo spotted Dad in his usual waterproof golf clothing, picking up his golf bag and folding golf cart, which could mean only one thing; Dad was off to do whatever it was you do at golf.

To make matters worse, Solo knew no matter how much he hinted that he wanted to come along, he wouldn't be allowed to do so. Solo was also aware that on this particular day, Dad would be playing in some kind of golf tournament, whatever that was. This gave Solo even more of an incentive to try to tag along.

However, given the horrible weather, his family had begged off coming, although Mum had said, "I will probably be along later."

Dad was quite relieved that his family wasn't coming to watch him play. This was his first club tournament, and he didn't need the extra pressure of trying to perform well in front of his family. Still, he was slightly disappointed nonetheless. What if he played well? What if he actually won?

Suddenly images of him winning swirled through his head. The grand, silver trophy presented to him by the club chairman. Applause and congratulations from his fellow club members.

For a brief moment, Dad thought winning might be a real possibility, but then he shook his head. It was not going to happen. He let out a small sigh. So it was just as well his family wasn't coming after all. What he didn't know was that Mum and the kids were going to show up later as a surprise to cheer him on, even if he didn't win, and even in the wet and dreary weather. All this was to come much later in the day.

As Dad got himself ready, he glanced down and saw Solo. "Solo! It's no good looking at me with those big, black eyes. I'm sorry you can't come. I'll see you later."

But Solo wasn't asking Dad to take him. He had other ideas.

As he had watched Dad get ready, Solo noticed that, as usual, Dad had left the rear hatch of the SUV open, ready to take the golf clubs and cart. Solo knew he could never get away with jumping in. Dad would spot him immediately. But Solo noticed another way. For whatever reason, Dad had left a rear side-door open. This was all the encouragement Solo needed.

Without waiting to think through the consequences of his actions, Solo jumped up, into the open rear door, and lay flat on the seat, trusting that Dad wouldn't notice a large, very white dog laying across the back seat of his car. As has been explained many times, Solo is a very optimistic dog.

Yet amazingly, for once, Solo's plan actually worked. Dad was in such as hurry to make it to the golf course on time that he simply rushed past the open door, closed it with a slam, put the car in gear, and drove off through the dreary drizzle.

Solo couldn't believe his luck. He lay as still as he could for the first ten minutes of the drive, but then temptation got the better of him. He wanted to see where they were going and do some people watching. If there was one thing Solo liked, apart from naps, walks, eating and hanging out with his family, it was people watching as they drove along. So he pushed himself up on his front legs and looked out the rain-splattered window, quite forgetting that Dad wasn't supposed to know he was there.

As Solo stared out the window, Dad looked in the car's rearview mirror and couldn't believe his eyes. "Solo!" he exclaimed for the second time that day. "How on earth...?" His voice died away as he swerved to avoid driving the car into a ditch.

Dad attempted to compose himself and kept driving, every once in a while looking in his rearview mirror just to make sure he wasn't seeing things and that really was Solo sitting directly behind him and grinning happily the whole time. What was he supposed to do now? He couldn't drive home; he would be late for the match. As they continued towards the club, Dad's mind was racing about what he was going to do with Solo. Solo, though, was quite content to be in Dad's company, even if all they were doing was driving together.

Eventually Dad pulled into the long drive of the golf club, parked, and immediately got out. He opened the rear door and stared at Solo. "Solo, I don't know how you managed to pull that off, but don't think for one minute that I am pleased with this."

Solo simply smiled at Dad and placed a paw on Dad's arm. Dad's anger subsided as fast as it had risen. After all, this was his fault. He should have known that Solo was eager to come and might try a trick like this. Dad could never be angry at Solo for very long. After all, Solo was *his* dog.

"Still, what are we going to do with you, Solo?" said Dad as he pondered the situation. Dad was due on the practice range, and then a round of golf which could take up to four hours. He couldn't leave Solo in the SUV all that time, even if it was a cold and dreary day.

Dad made up his mind. One of the girls who worked in the reception area of the club would take care of Solo. Solo made friends easily, and the girls were bound to "ooh" and "ahh" over Solo. People often did. It was a trait that Solo would milk to perfection in the form of tummy and head rubs.

Dad decided he would offer a good tip to the girls to make sure Solo was taken care of. Besides, Solo would enjoy meeting new people as he waited.

As Dad surmised, the two girls on duty at the reception desk immediately fell in love with Solo and were more than delighted to take care of him as he seemed to be such a well-behaved dog. Dad may have bent the truth a little on that one. That and the large tip Dad had promised at the end of the tournament were enough to convince the girls.

Solo was given pride of place next to the reception area, and a large bowl of ice-cold water was provided for him also. As Dad had guessed, Solo was quite content to watch all the comings and goings from the golf club. The girls had even promised to take Solo for a walk in an hour or so.

Pleased that he had managed to solve a short-term crisis even though it meant parting with some cash, Dad went over to the driving range to get warmed up for his match. After about thirty minutes of practice, it was Dad's turn to tee off. Dad was relieved his family wasn't there to see him hit his first ball of the match. He was extremely nervous and was sure he would make a fool of himself in front of his fellow players.

For a split second, Dad was wondering why he wasn't still in bed on this miserable Saturday morning, but he put all thoughts other than hitting the ball straight and true out of his mind. He took a deep breath, swung, and hit. The ball sailed majestically, exactly where he had intended it to go. The small crowd of onlookers gave a polite clap. Dad allowed himself a little smile.

The rest of the match went very well, and Dad was in top form. The group of four he was playing in made their way to the final, eighteenth tee. Dad was tied for first place. This was it. All he had to do was win this hole, and Dad would win the tournament.

He already had visions of holding the cup high above his head, other club members offering to buy him drinks, and the surprised look on the faces of his family when he arrived home with a silver cup that was larger than Solo was tall.

Once again, Dad hit a perfect shot down the fairway. *One shot down, four to go,* thought Dad.

Meanwhile back at the clubhouse, Solo was getting impatient. The novelty of watching all the club members and their friends and family coming to and fro had worn off hours before. While the girls had promised to take Solo for a walk, they had totally forgotten about him once some of the younger, male players had shown up.

All in all, Solo was left to his own devices. And Solo the Dog left to his own devices is not necessarily a good thing.

Solo wandered around, quite unhindered by any member of the club. They had all met Solo as they entered the club and knew he was a good dog, quite capable of taking care of himself, and certainly no harm to anyone. As he wandered through the lounge, some club members even ruffled his head and asked him to shake. Solo was only too happy to oblige.

Other members of the club were watching the match through the large windows of the clubhouse as Dad's group of four came down the fairway. Solo watched too. And even from this distance, Solo could see Dad's silhouette. Solo recognized Dad's blue golf jacket too. Now this was exactly what Solo had come here to do: to understand exactly what golf was and, more importantly, to see Dad doing it.

Solo wandered over to one of the open doors that led out to the patio area of the clubhouse. No one else was out there as the weather was too inhospitable. Solo was too far away to see much, but in the distance, he could see that Dad was using a large stick to hit a small white ball.

Solo needed to be closer. How could he learn about golf from such a distance? This was totally unreasonable, to be expected to observe golf from so far away. Although, why anyone would want to use a large, funny stick to hit a small, white ball was beyond him. Why not simply pick the ball up in your mouth?

Dad was feeling confident. If he was able to get the ball into the hole with just two more shots, he would win. Once again visions of great triumph danced through his mind. He shook his head to clear those thoughts. It was too soon to assume victory. Make these shots, and *then* he could do his victory dance, he thought.

Dad lined up to hit the ball to the green as another player hit a perfect shot that landed close to the hole. Dad would have to make this one count or he would lose. He took his stance and hit the best shot of his life. He knew even before it landed that he would have an easy putt to win the match and the tournament.

Meanwhile, Solo had made his way towards the final hole. He stood on a small rise overlooking the green, his large, white body clearly visible to everyone in the clubhouse.

"Is that a dog?" someone watching from the clubhouse asked.

"I wonder if he's a member," said another.

A third said, "I wonder what his handicap is?" There was a general chuckling all around from the spectators.

Solo arrived just in time to see the shot hit by the player before Dad land on the green and roll to within five feet of the hole. This puzzled Solo to no end. Surely the objective was to get the ball *in* the hole, not close to it.

Dad was too engrossed in watching his ball sail gracefully through the air and land within two feet of the hole to notice Solo. The match was now his to lose. Make this easy putt and greatness would be thrust upon him. He allowed himself a little dance to celebrate.

Solo watched the ball land and was disappointed for Dad. It hadn't landed *in* the hole. Solo decided that he would do something about this. Assuming, quite incorrectly, that no one would notice a large, white, and very wet dog walk across the green, he wandered over to Dad's ball, gently picked it up, and popped it neatly into the hole. Then, sitting back on his haunches by the flag with a huge self-satisfied grin on his face, he waited to be congratulated by Dad.

One of Dad's foursome walked up to him and said, "Isn't that your dog?"

Dad, who had not been paying attention up until that point, squinted through the rain. "Solo!" he muttered to himself. "Now what?"

Back at the clubhouse, Solo's antics had been observed by the club members and their friends and family who had been watching from behind the large windows. Amazed at Solo's antics, everyone braved the rain to go out to the patio and give Solo a huge round of applause.

At that very moment, Solo's other family members showed up. Mum and the kids joined the crowd, thinking they were applauding the winner and hoping it was Dad. But instead of seeing Dad raising his hands in victory, they saw Solo beside the flag with his massive grin of satisfaction.

"Mum, it's Solo," the kids cried.

Mum groaned and attempted to hide.

One member of the audience turned to Mum. "Is that your dog?"

Mum nodded and said, "Regretfully, yes. What has he done now?"

"He scored a hole in one."

Mum couldn't believe her ears. How on earth did Solo manage to do that?

As much as Mum couldn't believe her ears, Dad couldn't believe his eyes. Where had his ball gone? He and his playing buddies wandered onto the green. There were three balls visible. Dad knew he hadn't made the hole, so where was his ball?

He got closer and looked down into the hole. Sure enough, there was his ball. And sure enough, there was Solo, eyes dancing in delight at the thought of helping Dad win!

A few days later, anyone visiting the golf clubhouse would find, near the end of the rows upon rows of photographs of member achievements, a picture of Dad holding the large cup for winning the most recent tournament. At the very end of the row, however, they would find, hanging for all the world to see, a picture of Solo, sitting on his haunches with a big grin on his face. Under the picture, a brass engraving said, "To Solo the Dog, for outstanding sportsmanship, we award the title of Honorary Member."

Then quite naturally, to round this off and to Dad's even greater embarrassment, the picture of Solo made the front page of the local newspaper with the headline "Hole in One!"

"Solo," said Dad, as he stared at the newspaper, "how many more times are you going to make the headlines?"

Solo looked at him in a way that seemed to say that he had absolutely no idea.

2. Solo Mends the Road

One hot, sticky day, a water main burst on Solo's street. The force of the water ripped out large chunks of road and provided Solo and the children with hours of entertainment by giving them access to their own personal fountain. They jumped through the water. They lay on their stomachs over the jet to see if they could float a few feet above the ground, which, it turned out, they couldn't. They made small, paper boats and raced them down the street in their own private stream to see who could win by getting to the drain first.

Solo did not make paper boats, but he did have just as much fun as the children by barking encouragement at the boats as they floated down the street and, of course, by simply running through the water as often as he wanted.

All in all, the younger members of Solo's family felt the burst water pipe made for a very good day indeed. Mum and Dad didn't think the water main break was much fun, though, as they had to forgo any baths, showers, or even making a cup of tea or coffee.

Dad made a decision. "As nothing can be done until the pipe is fixed, I might as well go to the golf club."

Mum raised an eyebrow. "What's to be done is dealing with soaking wet kids and a very wet and dirty dog."

But all good things must end, and the water company repaired the pipe, much to the annoyance of Solo and the children, who felt that left unrepaired, a broken pipe could lead to many more hours and days of water adventures. Once the pipe was fixed, the next job was repairing the road.

Soon enough a crew was soon along to patch the hole in the road. The workers would simply fill the hole with hot tar that, once cool, would leave a durable, but not necessarily smooth, surface.

Dad was not happy about this solution right outside his house. He asked the foreman of the repair crew if they could patch the hole with much more durable concrete as the plan to simply use tar would leave an uneven surface right where he would turn into his drive.

The supervisor informed Dad that this was just how things were done, and if he wanted a better solution, he would have to take the issue up with his boss. But as Dad was about to leave to the golf club and knew full well that his argument would be futile, Dad simply waved his arms in disgust and went back inside to grab his golf clubs.

As the workers first used a large machine to rip out unwanted debris, then began to pour a hot, steaming black ooze into the hole, Solo was watching from the window in anticipation, hoping that something extraordinary would take place, but it didn't. This was simply a hole in the road being repaired.

Solo, being Solo, became bored. What had seemed interesting at first provided Solo with no entertainment whatsoever after a few minutes, so he decided to head into the back garden to see if anything exciting was happening there. Perhaps on the way to the back garden another member of the family might take pity on him and offer to take him for a walk. Solo, as has been noted many times, is a highly optimistic dog.

As he wandered through the house attempting to look sorrowful for any family member he might come across, not one family member paid him any attention. He could hear the daughter playing with her friends upstairs, which meant Solo needed to stay well clear lest he be forced to wear a pink tutu and a gold crown again.

As he neared the back of the house, he could hear the son yelling at the TV, which could only mean one thing: he was playing video games. Solo knew from experience that he would never get a walk from the son if he were playing video games. Solo had tried on many occasions to get the boy's attention when he was engrossed in shooting some alien or another, but each time he had been unceremoniously and brutally rebuffed.

Solo had even tried to gain the boy's attention with a paw on the knee and an eager look in the eyes, a tactic guaranteed to get a reaction from most humans. This had failed to work on the boy, who told him, "Go away, Solo. You're blocking my view," while pushing Solo off his knees.

So Solo kept going, hoping for better luck in the back of the house. Perhaps Mum would take him for a walk. But Mum wasn't in the kitchen. She was in the sitting room talking to some friends, drinking coffee and having some cake. This was the book club, which met once a week to discuss anything to do with literature.

Solo knew that when Mum was with her friends, laughing and chatting like this, the odds of getting a walk, or any attention for that matter, were extremely remote. Still, he might just get lucky if he looked cute enough. So putting on his best wide-eyed innocent look, Solo pushed the half-open door all the way and walked into the sitting room.

Solo knew that people would generally make a fuss over him, especially visitors as they did not have to put up with any of his adventures, which his family were all too familiar with. So as he wandered into the sitting room, Solo had no doubt that someone from the book club might play with him. But Solo also knew from bitter experience that no matter how much fuss a visitor might make of him, within a minute Mum would grow tired of Solo's presence and force him to leave.

Mum knew far more than most how Solo could cause trouble, even if by accident, and she would not take a chance with her book club, which she was trying to impress with her knowledge of Charles Dickens. Mum, seeing Solo's attempt to ingratiate himself with the group, stood up, grabbed him by the collar, and forced him out the door, closing it firmly behind him.

Solo looked at the closed door for a few seconds, feeling slightly dejected, but hearing the birds sing outside and knowing the whole world was there just for him, he decided to move on in search of adventure. But as he wandered out the back door and into the garden, Solo began to feel dejected again as nothing remotely interesting seemed to be taking place. He wandered around for a few minutes, then, once more hearing the men working on the road out front, decided the best course of action was to see what they were up to. Maybe *they* would play with him.

Solo walked up the drive towards the street, but was dismayed to find the workers had all gone. Their truck, their digger—everything had all seemed to vanish in a matter of seconds. All that remained was a patch of black goo near the side of the road with a few cones around it to keep drivers from getting too close. Once again denied any excitement, Solo turned around and started to walk back down the drive, as clearly this was one of those days when nothing interesting ever, ever was going to happen.

But suddenly it did! As he turned the corner around the side of the house, Solo literally ran head-first into a squirrel. Solo had not been paying attention. The squirrel, who was rummaging for nuts, had also not been paying attention.

There they stood, two archenemies, literally with their noses touching, so surprised to see each other at such close range that neither seemed quite sure what to do next. For a few more seconds, they eyed each other, dog and squirrel, squirrel and dog, until, slowly, Solo's eyes narrowed and a long, low growl emanated from his lips.

The squirrel knew from their previous encounters that it was much faster than Solo, but it was so surprised that it spent a moment or two trying to figure out its first move. However, when Solo started to growl, the squirrel decided enough was enough. Having been chased by Solo too many times to let this opportunity pass, it leaned forward slightly, opened its mouth to show a row of razor-sharp teeth, and bit Solo hard on the nose.

Solo let out a yelp and backed away, giving the squirrel just enough time to make its next move, running directly between Solo's front legs and emerging past his tail. The squirrel was so fast that all Solo could manage was to look down between his legs, just in time to see the squirrel scampering away as fast as it could towards the front of the house.

Taken aback for a few seconds, Solo wasn't sure which way to turn as he was reeling from the pain of his bitten nose, but finally took off after the squirrel, which, having gained a good head start, ran as fast as it could towards the road. Solo's throbbing nose seemed to give him more speed than normal, and with a few massive leaps, soon Solo wasn't too far from the squirrel's tail. Solo was determined to repay the squirrel for the sore nose by giving the squirrel a sore bottom.

Sensing Solo was closing in fast, the squirrel accelerated and turned onto the road...and directly into the muddy ooze from the road repair. The thick goo soon slowed the squirrel down to such an extent that it was barely moving at all, like running in molasses. Only a few inches from making it to the other side of the tar, the squirrel became completely stuck. With both rear legs in the tar, try as it might, it couldn't move.

Solo, seeing the squirrel stopped, but not interested in wondering why, plowed ahead. Unlike the squirrel, who was too small to hit the yellow warning tape tied between the cones, Solo ran directly into the tape, which wrapped around his neck, and as he kept running, Solo pulled a few of the yellow and red warning cones with him.

Solo could see he was gaining fast on the squirrel, who was still struggling to emancipate himself from the goop, but as he got closer, Solo realized the squirrel was stuck and that he might get stuck too. Trying desperately to avoid the same fate, Solo braced both front paws in an attempt to slow down, but it was too little too late. He was in the tar.

Very quickly, even a dog of Solo's strength could not move. Solo was stuck in a part-running, part-trying-to-stop position that placed him within inches of the squirrel. If Solo had chosen to stick out his tongue at this point, he could have reached the squirrel's tail; that's how close he was.

Solo's attempts at getting out of the tar were not successful. First, he tried lifting one paw, then another, but this only had the effect of pushing down any of his paws which were still in the tar. The more he struggled, the more stuck he became.

Solo found this very disconcerting. Here he was, literally within inches of his major foe, and he couldn't do anything about it. Slowly it dawned on him that he was going to need help getting out. Besides, he was getting hungry. It had to be near dinner time, and he was growing tired of this game.

Solo started to howl. The squirrel started to chatter. The more they struggled, the more bogged down they became, and the more bogged down they became, the more the squirrel chattered and the more Solo howled.

"What on earth is that racket?" said Mum as she put down her cup of tea. She was really annoyed as she was about to give what she felt would be a great dissertation and unique view on the collective works of Charles Dickens, and the commotion coming from the road outside had interrupted the little speech she had worked on for weeks.

28

Followed closely by her curious book club, she walked up the drive towards the road, not sure exactly what was going on. As she got closer though, she began to recognize the high-pitched barking sound as Solo's. This was the bark Solo had perfected recently that guaranteed the best attention from his family. He would use this if he wanted a walk, or to be fed, or to be let back in the house. Overall, his family found the bark extremely annoying.

"What has that dog been up to now?" muttered Mum as she turned onto the road.

Whatever Mum had expected to see had not prepared her for what she actually *did* see. There was Solo, still stuck in the drying tar with some yellow warning tape wrapped around his neck and two traffic cones trailing behind. In front, a squirrel, against all odds, was making its way slowly out of the ooze, leaving a line of small paw prints.

Mum rubbed her eyes in disbelief. "What on earth...?" was all she could manage as her book club friends gathered around her. With her mouth wide open, all Mum could do was stare in disbelief at the state of affairs outside her house. Wonderment at Solo's predicament slowly gave way to embarrassment, as she knew it wouldn't be long before her gossipy book club friends would have this story all over the village.

Mum had barely even noticed the squirrel, focused as she was on Solo, until, with a major effort, it managed to leap clear of the tar. Pausing just long enough to give Solo a scornful look, then chattering loudly at the entire gathering of Solo and the book club, it took off towards its nest in one the trees in Solo's back garden.

Mum's fellow book club members started to giggle as it dawned on them what had happened. Mum could feel her face going red with embarrassment thinking this day couldn't get any worse, until it did.

A passing police car stopped, parking in the road to prevent other cars from passing. Putting on the flashing blue lights, two officers got out to check on the situation. Eventually a line of cars formed, some with small children in the back, many of which pointed at Solo. Several people took pictures on their phones.

Mum kept urging the policemen to do something, but they were as confused as Mum on the best course of action. With a yell of frustration, partially at the police, and partially because she felt she couldn't listen to Solo's whiny bark any longer, Mum decided she couldn't wait any longer.

Muttering to herself, "Why did we ever get a dog?" and with prompting from her book club, Mum stepped into the tar and, with a Herculean effort, managed to help Solo out of the black goo. Unfortunately, even though she was able to get Solo out, Mum had forgotten to remove her new expensive shoes, which came off her feet as she stepped onto firm ground. The shoes became a new and permanent fixture of the road.

This, then, was the sight that greeted the road repair crew when they returned the next day to remove the cones and tape: a pair of woman's shoes, half-buried in the tar; a trail of paw prints, large and small; and two traffic cones firmly buried in the hard tar, from which some yellow tape blew in the breeze. The road crew felt that someone had played a joke on them, but they had no idea who.

Joke or not, this meant the crew had to dig up the road, rip out the shoes and cones, and once more fill in the hole. This time, they used quick drying concrete, just in case someone else came along and thought it would be hilarious to throw old shoes into the repair.

When Dad returned that day, he heard all about Solo's misadventures from his wife, who reminded him yet again that Solo was *his* first choice for a dog, not hers. She also told her husband that she would be buying a new pair of expensive shoes and that he wasn't to complain when he saw her credit card bill. Dad opened his mouth to say something, but catching a withering look from his wife, decided it was best to remain silent.

That evening, when taking Solo for a walk, Dad noticed that the repair in the road was patched with smooth, white concrete, just as he had originally asked for. It dawned on him that Solo was responsible for this state of affairs, even if it had meant his wife had to buy another pair of shoes. So later that night, after Dad had taken Solo on a particularly long walk as a reward and when his wife had gone to bed, he gave Solo one of his favorite treats, one shaped like a huge bone.

As Solo chowed down on this giant treat from his favorite spot in the kitchen, Dad leaned over and patted Solo on the head, quietly whispering in Solo's ear, "Man's best friend indeed, Solo."

3. Solo and the Carpenter

Solo was going for his evening walk with Dad. The route consisted of starting down the road outside their house, then right to the next road, then cut through some fields, and back around to home. Solo liked walking with Dad. After all, it was Dad who had found Solo at the Dog Rescue, and it was Dad who had named him.

Unfortunately, the novelty of having to walk Solo had long since worn off for the rest of the family. Part of the deal of getting a dog in the first place was that everyone would take turns walking Solo. Unfortunately, the children, who really loved Solo, were always able to bring up valid excuses as to why they couldn't walk Solo: "too much homework" or "stupid piano lessons, Dad." His wife wasn't much help either, as she often had to "help the kids with their homework" or "drive the kids to tennis lessons." So, many times as not, it fell to Dad to take Solo for his evening walk.

As they walked down the road away from their house, Dad wondered, not for the first time, why it was that his entire family, who claimed to love Solo, rarely found the time to walk him. "Don't I have other things to do too?" said Dad under his breath. He really wanted to keep working on his old sports car, which he had purchased as a replacement for the motorcycle he had been forced to sell after an unfortunate—and embarrassing—incident that quite naturally included Solo.

Still, he had to admit, as walks go this wasn't too bad. It was a nice, warm evening. The birds were singing, and as Solo knew the route as well as Dad, Solo wasn't even on a lead. He simply trotted beside Dad, stopping every once in a while to smell something—usually something quite disgusting.

As they came to a curve in the road, Dad and Solo heard the sound of a hammer banging on nails. Then the unmistakable yell of someone who had missed the nail and hit their fingers instead. Dad stopped and looked over the old gate that led into the local soccer field. A man was attempting to hammer a nail into a plank of wood on the side of an old shed that was used to store sports equipment. Dad opened the gate and walked over to him with Solo following closely, quite happy to leave their usual, designated route.

"Need some help?" said Dad as the man nursed his bruised thumb.

The man looked up, rubbing his hand. "Oh sure," he said. "Thanks. I can't hold the wood in place and hammer the nail in at the same time." Dad held the plank of wood where it needed to be placed while the carpenter hammered in a couple of nails. "Thanks again," said the man. "I can take it from here." He shook Dad's hand, then looked down and noticed Solo for the first time. "Well, aren't you a fine looking fellow?"

Solo, who was very polite, held out a paw for the man to shake.

"What needs doing?" asked Dad. "I know this shed is old, but it looks in reasonable shape."

"Well, several pieces of wood are rotten, so I was asked to do the work," said the man. "I'm a carpenter by trade, so this is easy work for me."

Dad didn't recognize the man, so he asked him where he was from. It turned out the man was down on his luck and was traveling from town to town and village to village looking for carpentry work. He told Dad his business had failed, and in order to keep costs low, he would get on his bike with a few tools and see what work he could scrounge up.

Dad and the carpenter spoke for about thirty minutes before Dad realized he needed to get home in time for supper. He gave the man his address and offered him some work on Dad's old workshop. Mum had been urging him to get the old structure spruced up.

"It has character," Dad had told her.

"It's embarrassing," said Mum.

Dad decided to get the work done after all.

As Dad walked home with Solo trotting beside him, Solo thought what a nice man the carpenter was. He was already looking forward to the next day when the carpenter would come to repair Dad's old workshop. Solo had made up his mind he was going to keep him company and, where possible, help out.

Solo liked to help his human friends. He was a very sociable dog and always knew he could lend a paw if needed. Solo went to bed that night excited about the prospect of learning how to become a carpenter.

The next day, the carpenter arrived bright and early on his old, somewhat rusty bicycle. Behind him, in a homemade trailer, he towed all his tools. The carpenter was clearly extremely proud of his tools. While the saws, hammers, and other instruments of the carpenter's trade were old, they were very well taken care of, not a patch of rust on anything. The edges of his various handsaws gleamed with sharpness in the equally sharp, early-morning sunshine.

Dad and Solo went outside to meet him. Dad spent a few minutes showing the carpenter around his old workshop and where he felt repairs were needed. Then, explaining it was Sunday and that he was late for his game of golf, he left the carpenter in the company of Solo and departed.

Solo watched in fascination as the carpenter removed the tools he would need. Dad had already set aside some wood for the repair work, so the carpenter pulled out a well-used, folding workbench, his hammers, some nails and screws which were in an old-fashioned, crown paper bag, and of course his trusty saws. Removing his tape measure from his work belt, the carpenter set about measuring Dad's workshop for the needed repairs.

Solo followed him diligently, and the carpenter didn't mind one iota. Dad was not exactly the world's greatest handyman. In fact, Solo had yet to see Dad repair or fix anything, let alone use a saw and hammer. So all this to-ing and fro-ing by the carpenter fascinated Solo to no end.

"How are you this morning, Solo?" the carpenter asked as he set about removing a particularly rotten piece of wood from the side of the workshop.

Solo looked at him in a way which he hoped communicated, "Just great, thank you."

The carpenter, looking at Solo, seemed to interpret the look well. "Pleased to hear it, Solo. Now, what do you think? Should we replace all this section of the workshop, or just this portion?" He pointed to a well-rotted side of the workshop. He looked at Solo. "I agree. All of it. We must do a good job, Solo. Agreed?" He stuck out his hand, and on instinct Solo stuck out his paw, which the carpenter shook.

After that, Solo and the carpenter became firm friends. Solo would follow the carpenter around as he carried his tools, sawed wood, and banged in nails with his trusty hammer. When lunchtime came, Solo lay down next to the carpenter as he leaned against the wheel of his battered, old trailer and ate the sandwiches he had bought with him.

Mum came out and offered the carpenter some fresh water. She also placed a bowl down for Solo. "Is he bothering you?" she asked.

"Of course not," came the reply. "I enjoy the company, actually." He patted Solo on the head. Naturally Solo moved closer to make it easier for the carpenter to pat him some more.

The rest of the repairs went well, although that evening, as Dad paid the carpenter for the day's work, they both realized that the work was going to take longer than anticipated as Dad had let his workshop fall into quite a poor state. So it was no surprise that the carpenter would have to come back the following day to finish. Solo was quite pleased about this idea. He felt he was learning quite a lot about carpentry.

The next day was even hotter than the day before, and the carpenter was sweating heavily as he started to saw the replacement sections of wood to the right size. Solo was quite content to lay down in the shade and watch him work. Soon, though, the carpenter decided he needed a nice, cool drink, so he fetched a cold drink from his old wagon and sat down on the ground, leaning against one of the wheels.

Solo fancied a nice, cool drink too. And even though Mum had set his water bowl down on the driveway for him, Solo decided that whatever the carpenter was drinking was no doubt superior to the water Mum had given him. So he got up, walked over to the carpenter, and looked longingly at the man's water bottle.

Not needing another hint, the carpenter leaned away from the wheel slightly, holding up the bottle, tilted it slightly, and allowed the water to slowly drain out. Solo stuck out his big tongue to lap it up. He decided this was the best water he'd ever tasted.

As the carpenter lay back against the wheel, there was a loud groan from the old cart. Ever so slowly, the wheel on the other side of the cart buckled and then collapsed. The cart tilted to one side and rested on top of the broken wheel. The carpenter felt himself lean back too far and spilled water all over himself as he lost his balance.

As he got over his surprise, he quickly stood up and walked around to examine the broken wheel. He sighed to himself. Solo came over to inspect the damage.

"That's not good, Solo," said the carpenter. "Where am I going to get another wheel at short notice? This old cart has seen better days, lad." He stroked Solo's head absentmindedly. "I wish I could afford a new one. A new bike too, come to think about it. One that's easier on my hips. Oh well, there it is." He picked up the cart so as to get at the bent and broken wheel, removed it, and tossed it into the back of the cart, leaving the cart still tilted to one side.

That night when Dad came home from work, he looked at the craftsmanship the old carpenter had done on his workshop. He told his wife he wished he had more work for him, as the work was so good and that clearly, "The old-timer could use the money."

The carpenter peddled away on his old bicycle, promising to return in a day or so with a new wheel so he could tow his trailer away. As Solo lay on his bed that night, he thought about the old carpenter and wished, not for the first time, that he could help his human friends. Solo didn't know exactly what he could do, but he did know that he wanted to help the carpenter get not only a new trailer, but a new bike too. And as we know, Solo is a very determined and lucky dog.

The next day Solo awoke with absolutely no plan whatsoever to help the carpenter. Solo had often found that overthinking a problem would cause more problems than the actual problem itself. Instead, Solo found that leaving fate to solve his problem for him was often the best way to approach a situation.

Solo decided to go to the end of the drive and lay down in his favorite thinking spot. This was just off to the side of the drive, near the road, under a large tree. Here he could see anyone walking or driving by, but also keep an ear out for any interesting activity that might be going on in the house behind him. One thing Solo did not like was missing out on any interesting activity. If there was something exciting going on, then it wasn't really exciting enough unless Solo was involved.

As he lay down on the cool grass, his mind began to wander. The grass was just too cool, the shade from the tree just too perfect for him to stay focused on the problem. Instead, he felt his eyes begin to close, and he made up his mind that the best way to help the old carpenter was to take a nice, long nap. But just as his eyes were about to close, he saw a sight he had never seen before.

There, on the road in front of him, was an adult, riding what can only be described as a giant version of a child's tricycle. Solo had seen many children riding their small trikes, but never a grown-up on one.

This thing was spectacular to behold. It was bright red with large, shiny wheels. It had lights on the front and back. It even had a large, wicker basket hanging off the rear. And best of all, it was ridden by Solo's friend the vicar. Whether or not the vicar would consider Solo a friend is unclear, as no one has ever asked him.

The vicar always tried to steer clear of Solo ever since his first experience, when he was trapped, hanging on to the front of a car as Solo drove it into a pond. Yet he couldn't help but have a soft spot for Solo as, without him, the church steeple might have collapsed. None of this prevented the vicar from avoiding Solo wherever possible though.

The vicar was proud of his new mode of transportation. First, it meant he was less likely to fall off, something that had happened recently when he spotted Solo in the back of the family SUV and had driven his old, two-wheeled bike into a muddy ditch. Secondly, the large basket on the back allowed him to carry his weekly shopping from the local supermarket without having to balance oversize loads on the front of his old bike.

The vicar was in a good mood as he rode close to Solo's house. Normally any time he went by, he would keep a close eye out for Solo given his propensity to cause mayhem upon the vicar's person. But as he got closer, he failed to spot Solo, hidden as he was to the side of the drive. The vicar let out a deep sigh of relief.

When Solo first noticed the vicar on his shiny, new bike, he understood this was exactly the type of machine his new friend the carpenter needed. It was easy to ride, it had a large basket which could carry many tools, and it even had gears. Solo stood up in excitement as he wanted to examine this shiny, new machine in more detail. Without thinking, Solo ran out in to the street, directly in the path of the vicar and his bike.

Seeing a massive, white blur heading right for him, the vicar instinctively swerved to avoid hitting whatever it was. He turned too fast and too sharp, drove directly into the ditch alongside the road, and was thrown off into a small pool of muddy, brown water.

As he sat there in the muddy gunk, he looked up to see Solo's smiling face staring down at him. The vicar was getting quite fed up when a car slowed down. It was the bishop.

He looked down at the vicar from his open window. "Good heavens, Michael, whatever are you doing?" said the bishop. "Stop playing with that dog. It lowers the tone of the church." And with that, the bishop drove on.

The vicar stood up and attempted to wipe some of the mud off his clothes. Muttering under his breath, he hauled his now less-than-shiny bike out of the ditch. He was just wondering if it was against the rules of the church to throw mud at a dog when the carpenter walked up.

"Are you all right, vicar?" he said. "Here let me help with that."

He assisted the vicar in pulling the three-wheeled bike out of the ditch. "Wow, that's a fancy bike, no mistake," said the carpenter. "What I wouldn't give for one of these. I could fit my tools in the back, nice and proper. No question about that." He continued to look at the vicar's trike approvingly.

"Well, it serves a purpose," said the vicar as he still attempted to get the mud off. He was on his way to see a very nice young lady in the hope of asking her to the cinema, but that would clearly have to wait. He looked at Solo through narrow eyes. "It was that dog," he said, pointing at Solo, "He's always causing me trouble."

"Solo?" said the carpenter. "He's the best dog ever. Aren't you, Solo?" Solo stuck out a paw for the carpenter to shake. "Solo was helping me yesterday when the back of my old tool trailer collapsed. I really wish I could afford a new one. Something like your bike would be even better."

At that moment, Solo did something most humans found extremely uncomfortable. He stared directly into the vicar's eyes and maintained that stare without blinking. Solo was renowned in his house for being able to win any staring contest.

"Err," said the vicar, feeling Solo's unblinking stare bore into his brain. "Yes, thank you." He felt uncomfortable for two reasons. Firstly, he could tell the old carpenter's need was greater than his own, and secondly, Solo's unrelenting stare was starting to give him a headache. "Well, goodbye," said the vicar, as he rode away. "Thanks for your help."

He turned around to wave, but instead of waving, his eyes were immediately transfixed by Solo, who seemed to be saying, "He needs a bike like yours too." The vicar peddled away as fast as he could, a slight shiver running down his spine as he felt Solo's continued stare boring deep into his back.

That night, the vicar had a nightmare. He dreamed he had driven his bike into a ditch and Solo was there. Only this time, Solo simply stared at him the entire time. And no matter how hard the vicar tried, he couldn't get out of the ditch.

The vicar woke up in a pool of sweat. "It was just a dream," he told himself as he tried to go back to sleep.

The vicar found the thought of Solo visiting him in his sleep slightly unnerving. It was bad enough running into Solo from time to time when he was awake. The thought of meeting Solo in his dreams too was absolutely horrifying.

The next day, the vicar couldn't get the carpenter and Solo out of his mind. He rang up the bishop and told him he would like to buy the carpenter a three-wheeled bike, just like his own, using church funds. The bishop agreed, although he did hope the carpenter would do a better job at riding his bike than the vicar did with his.

The following week, Solo made the front page of the local newspaper yet again. The picture showed the smiling carpenter being presented with a shiny, three-wheeled bike by the vicar. A large, red bow was fixed to the handlebars. The vicar though, while trying to smile, had his eyes turned slightly to one side.

For there was Solo, sitting once again on his rear, staring directly at the vicar. His look seemed to say, "Well done, vicar."

4. Solo's Big Break

It all started because a friend of a friend had heard about Solo's good looks and had reached out to Mum to see if the family would agree to a suggestion.

When she had told Dad about the proposal, his immediate response was an emphatic, "No! Solo in a TV studio. Could you imagine the carnage he would cause? It simply doesn't bear thinking about."

The friend of a friend was in the market for a dog to appear in a TV commercial for a new brand of dog food and felt that Solo would fit the bill perfectly.

Mum was very excited about the prospect as she told her husband, "Who do we know that can say they have a pet on TV? No one?" The more she thought about it, the more excited she became.

Dad, on the other hand, felt the more he thought about it, the more nervous he became. "It's all very well these people thinking Solo would be right for the part, but they don't have to live with him. I do. I know what that dog is capable of. All that expensive equipment…" His voice trailed off. Dad sat down hard in the most comfortable chair in the living room and rubbed his eyes. A nightmare of recrimination would surely follow any appearance by Solo in a studio. "We can't afford to pay for a new TV studio," Dad told his wife, who simply told him to stop being dramatic.

She would be there to make sure nothing bad was going to happen. What could possibly go wrong? Besides, hadn't there been the same concerns when Solo was a therapy dog in a hospital?

"You were for it; I wasn't," she reminded her husband. "Now you're against this? Why?"

"We were lucky," said Dad. "There were kids. Solo loves kids. This is different."

His wife cut him off. "Besides, the money would come in handy and could be used to pay for a new dress I have my eyes on."

Seeing his wife had made up her mind for him, Dad let out a groan and decided to go play some golf instead.

Before the big day, the family was sent a copy of the script by the agency. The script described how a young, presumably single woman had to leave her dog alone during the day. The dog would be sad, and even though he was happy to see his owner come home, he would only truly forgive her when she gave him a serving of his favorite dog food.

All Solo had to do was run around the set, look out of a window into a rainy day, waiting for his owner, and then when she did come home, run up to her, wagging his tail. Then when the young woman gave Solo his food, he would wag his tail even more furiously. The final shot would be of the woman and Solo on the couch watching television together.

Even Dad had to admit that this seemed easy enough, even for a "troublemaker" like Solo.

"Don't call him that," said Mum, stroking Solo's head. "You'll hurt his feelings."

Dad grunted and said from behind his newspaper, "It might work. Solo will do just about anything for food."

Soon Solo's big day arrived. In order to be ready for his close-up, he had been scrubbed within an inch of his life. His coat had been groomed, his nails cut, and even his tail had been trimmed. Solo felt he had undergone many indignities in his young life, but being prepared for the TV commercial was surely the worst.

Then to add insult to injury, he was confined to the house prior to leaving for the studio. Mum had learned a long time ago to never let Solo out after a bath as the first thing he would do is go and lay in the largest puddle he could find.

Solo had heard all the talk among the family of "Solo the TV star" or "Solo the Actor", but he had no idea what that meant. All he knew was that he had been taken out of his favorite spot by the warm stove in the kitchen, scrubbed and polished, and was now in the back of the family SUV on his way to who-knew-where.

He did get the sense that the entire family was excited—even Dad had come around somewhat—and eventually curiosity got the better of Solo, so he decided to make the best of the situation. Whatever this "commercial" thing was, it might turn out to be fun after all. Maybe, just maybe, they might have tennis balls for him to play with. Solo, as we know, was always a highly optimistic dog.

It wasn't too long before they arrived at the small studio where the commercial was to be shot. Solo jumped out of the car and Mum had a firm grip on his lead. She had learned one too many times that failing to hold on to the lead tight enough could lead to catastrophe.

They were met by a young woman who explained what was to happen during the day, and as Solo was not needed until the last part of the shoot, they could simply watch from behind the cameras. They went into the studio where a set of a living room and a kitchen had been built, along with a prop of a window which was to be sprayed with water as Solo looked out to make it appear like he was waiting for his owner to come home and staring into the rain.

The director came over, spoke briefly to Mum, then bent down and spoke gently to Solo. "This is your big break, Solo. If this works well, we can use you again. So please be the good dog I know you are." He then left to start filming the pieces with the young woman.

Solo watched with interest from his position on the floor behind the cameras. Every so often the director would shout, "Action," and everyone would stop talking and the young actress would go through her few lines without Solo. Soon enough Solo was needed on camera. Practicing the first scene was easy enough; the young woman would say goodbye to Solo at the door, and he would go and look out the 'rainy window' to wait for her return. Every time Solo did something right, he was given a treat as a reward, which he found to be most satisfying indeed.

The director shouted, "Action," cameras started to film, and the young actress stroked Solo's head and said she would be back soon. As she closed the door, Solo was supposed to stay behind, and then they would film him looking out of the window.

Unfortunately, as the woman had made such a fuss of Solo, he decided he wanted more, so instead of staring at the now closed door, Solo would simply walk around the fake wall to find his new friend. "This is a strange house," thought Solo, as he heard the director yell, "Cut, go again." Again they shot the scene, and again Solo simply walked around the fake wall holding the door.

This happened five more times before the director started to get impatient. "Who got this dog?" he said to no one in particular.

Solo couldn't understand what the shouting was about. A nice, young woman had made a fuss of him, and all he was doing was following her around a fake wall so he could get more attention. Eventually it was decided that Mum would be just off camera and say, "Stay," to Solo in order to make him keep staring long enough at the closed door in order to get the scene. Another ten takes later, they had the shot.

The director rubbed his hand through his hair. "This had better work," he said under his breath.

Mum had brought Solo's water bowl, so during a break, she filled it with water and placed it next to him. It was hot under the studio lights, and Solo decided acting was thirsty work, so he drank the whole thing. Mum filled up the bowl again, and again Solo drank the whole thing.

The next scene was of Solo staring out of the rain-spattered window, looking for his owner. This scene was shot in one take as Mum was placed off-camera, facing Solo on the other side of the glass, and telling Solo to 'stay'.

"Perhaps this won't be so bad after all," said the director to no one in particular.

The next scene was when the owner came home and fed Solo his favorite food. This went off without a hitch, until Solo decided he didn't like the dog food and spat it out.

"Good grief," said the director. "The dog doesn't like the food."

They tried again, and again Solo refused to eat it. But then at the suggestion of Mum, they added some bacon to the food, and Solo ate it right down. "I must remember not to buy this food for Solo," Mum thought.

Now the final scene was set. This would be the simplest of the day. Solo and his young owner would be watching TV together. Solo was to be positioned on the couch, his head resting on the woman's knee as she ate some popcorn. Then as the woman was eating the popcorn, Solo would look enviously at her, decide he's hungry too, and get off the couch in order to lick up any remaining dog food in his bowl in the kitchen. Finally, a voice would say, "Doggo Dog Food is so good, your dog will even give up TV for it."

Well, that was the plan anyway. All Solo had to do was to lay on the couch, his head on the woman's knee, then when commanded by Mum, he was to go into the kitchen to eat some scraps in the bowl, which had been primed with bacon in order to encourage Solo to leave the couch.

With Solo and the actress positioned correctly on the couch, the director shouted, "Action," and the woman started to eat the popcorn.

Then Mum shouted, "Come, Solo," for Solo to get off the couch and eat the food.

The problem was that Solo really liked the smell of the popcorn. He was never allowed any at home. And he certainly didn't like the boring, old dog food they were giving him today, even if it did have bacon in it. So he ignored Mum's command. Instead, he lifted his large head and gently grabbed the bag of popcorn from the woman's hand.

Taken totally by surprise, she let it slip into Solo's mouth. He promptly ran off the couch with the bag of popcorn upside down. Then he ran behind the cameras, leaving a trail of popcorn as he went.

Finding a dark corner of the studio, Solo was disappointed to find that the popcorn bag was empty. Then looking behind him, and seeing the trail of popcorn on the floor, he slowly retraced his steps, stopping every once in a while to eat the fallen popcorn. It was as delicious as it smelled. But, just as Solo was about to grab another bite, he was unceremoniously interrupted when Mum grabbed him by the collar and dragged him back to the couch.

"Oh, Solo," she said. "All we need you to do is stay on the couch, then jump off when I tell you to. Please, Solo," Mum pleaded.

Solo's feelings were hurt. How was he supposed to focus when the delightful smell of popcorn was in the air? It all seemed too much for any dog to handle. Still, he had no choice. And having eaten as much of the fallen popcorn as he could, he went back to the couch, lay down, and rested his head on the knee of the actress as she ate from a *new* bag of popcorn.

"Okay, everyone," said the director. "Action!" The woman playing Solo's owner took a few bites of the popcorn, then Mum, off camera again, told Solo to jump down and walk towards the kitchen. The director said, "Cut," and that was that.

Now all they had to do was get set for the final scene. This time Solo would be filmed coming into the kitchen where he would take a mouthful of the food in the bowl, proving that the dog food was even more enticing to a dog than popcorn and TV. Which Solo knew was not true. But at least the food in the bowl was now laced with more bacon, something Solo could not resist.

While Solo was waiting for the crew to get ready for the next shot, he took advantage of no one watching him, sneaked over to the part of the studio where some thoughtful person had swept up the remaining popcorn, and scarfed it down. Then he decided for good measure to eat the entire contents of the bowl.

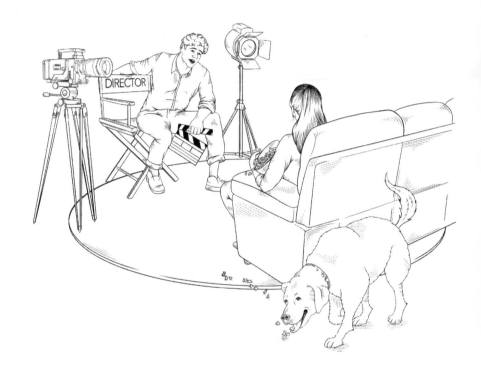

"Oh, Solo," said Mum, as the crew was forced yet again to fill the bowl with Doggo Dog Food and some extra bacon.

One of the crew members told the director they were now out of bacon, so this needed to be the correct take. The director hoped so, if only for his own sanity.

Eventually, everyone was ready. The cameras were ready. The lighting was ready. And Solo was ready.

The director shouted, "Action!" for what he hoped was the last time, and Solo was prompted by Mum to walk over to the dog food and take a bite or two.

Solo was starting to feel slightly unwell. He noticed that his stomach was doing some gyrations. Some of the food that Solo had eaten was starting to disagree with him. What with the dog food, then more dog food with bacon, then popcorn, then more dog food with bacon, then popcorn again, Solo knew something wasn't right. But he kept going. All he needed to do was to get to the bowl, take a bite, and then he would be on his way home, ready for a nice nap under the kitchen table.

With the cameras still whirring, Solo got closer to the bowl of food. Normally the smell of dog food, in particular the smell of dog food with bacon, would have caused Solo's mouth to water as he waited in anticipation to take his first bite. Unfortunately, this time the smell of the food had the opposite effect.

Solo began to feel distinctly nauseated. The effect of all the food and popcorn was now doing a number on his stomach. He made it to the bowl. As requested, he took a bite, a large bite. Solo didn't know how to eat in small doses.

The cameras captured every tasty morsel as Solo swallowed. Solo was supposed to take another large bite, but this time, Solo didn't want more. He didn't want more of anything. All he wanted to do was lie down a little and rest his head, which was now beginning to spin a little. But it was too late.

Within an instant, the food Solo had just eaten, and much more besides, no longer resided inside Solo. It was now spread over the floor of the studio in a very gooey and very smelly mess.

"Good grief," said the director as he hung his head.

"Oh, Solo!" said Mum. She and the entire crew looked away and covered their noses.

Solo, not quite sure why he felt the way he did, decided the best thing to do, after all, was lie down. But before that, as he made his way to the couch, he stopped right at the director's feet and deposited the rest of his stomach directly onto the director's new and extremely expensive Italian shoes.

"Oh no," Mum groaned.

The director couldn't believe it and simply stood there, the remains of Solo's stomach slowly dripping from his shoes. Solo, meanwhile, made it over to the coach, climbed up, and lay down with a satisfied sigh. This would help, he thought.

He was starting to feel better already. What Solo didn't realize, was that as he walked towards the pristine white coach, he was walking through the remains of his stomach, which he then deposited onto the couch.

"I'm *not* sitting on that couch again!" said the actress who played his owner.

Solo fell asleep immediately, but it wasn't long before he was woken up by Mum, who felt it was best to leave the studio as soon as possible. As he was led out, Solo noticed much of the crew using mops, and some kind of smelly sprays to help clean up Solo's mess and disguise its smell. Before they left, a man in a suit came over and handed Mum an envelope with payment for Solo's services.

Mum said, "Thank you," then quickly led Solo towards the door. As she did so, she caught the eye of the director. Holding his shoes and socks and making sure she was watching, he deposited them into a very large bin.

A few weeks later, Solo and his family were watching television when the commercial for Doggo Dog Food came on. The family cheered as Solo was seen acting his part.

Solo, from his usual position on the floor in front of the television, watched with interest. He couldn't understand the human fascination with giving dogs special food. All humans needed to do was give dogs some popcorn. Now that, thought Solo, would solve a lot of problems. What's more, he would *want* to be in that commercial.

5. Solo and the Election

Solo's family were all agog. The entire country was in the grip of a national election. Which party would win, and who would become leader of the country?

Dad could be found pontificating every day over breakfast, complaining to anyone who would listen that the current government was "a complete mess and deserves to be thrown out on their ear." The race was too close to call right up until the day of the election, with the press either supporting one side or the other. The children in the household were too young to vote, but even they were caught up with election fever as the television stations ran nothing but election coverage seemingly all the time.

Only Mum and Solo seemed immune to the deluge of election coverage. Mum because she felt "each side was as bad as the other", and Solo because he simply didn't care. After all, he was not allowed to vote, so why should the election be of any interest to him whatsoever? When dogs were allowed to vote, then he would pay attention.

Solo did try to follow what was being said at the kitchen table each morning from his usual perch near the wood-burning stove, but not so close that he overheated. From what Solo could make out, the current Prime Minister had decided to call an election that caught everyone by surprise. It also caught the entire county by surprise when some of the worst weather in a long time poured down buckets and buckets of rain. This made the election process a very wet one indeed. It also meant that on election day, most voters were going to the polls in the rain.

Dad had decided to take the late train to work on the day of the election so he and Mum could go and vote. Their polling station was in the next village over, which meant that they would have to drive through the pouring rain. The foul weather and the thought of the current Prime Minister being reelected put Dad in a foul mood. The children were glad when they had to go to school.

"What shall we do with Solo?" said Mum after the children had gone to catch their bus and she and Dad prepared to go vote. "Leave him here? Although he might he enjoy the ride. Wouldn't you, boy?" She spoke directly to Solo, who had at that moment decided to do an almighty stretch on the kitchen floor.

Laying on his side, Solo's stretches were a sight to behold. First, he would rub the side of his head on the floor. Then he would stretch out his front legs, then his hind legs, before bringing the whole exercise together in one, long stretch.

Dad simply made a grunting sound under his breath as he observed Solo's elongated stretch. Solo wagged his tail in acknowledgment that Dad was looking at him. His tail made a loud *thud, thud* on the tiled floor. Dad turned to head out.

Solo ran into the hallway just as Mum and Dad had opened the front door. Without stopping for a second, he ran to the rear of the family's SUV and waited in the rain, a big smile on his face, wagging his tail ferociously.

"Go on, Solo," Mum said as she opened up the reach hatch, and Solo jumped right in.

Dad simply grunted a third time. The rain dripping down his neck wasn't helping improve his mood. Neither was the prospect of the current government being reelected.

As they drove down the narrow, country lanes out of their village and into the countryside, Solo sat up and looked around from his vantage point in the back. Solo loved going for rides. He liked the sway of the car, the sights he would see, and the new smells. Today though, no one was walking anywhere. The rain was simply too bad.

Solo did see the young vicar on his bike, wrapped up in yellow rain gear, trying to get somewhere, looking utterly miserable as he endeavored to avoid the worst of the puddles. Solo liked the vicar, and he liked to think the vicar liked him despite once having taken the vicar for a ride on the front of the family car and depositing him into a muddy pond.

As they drove by, the vicar looked up, recognizing the family's silver SUV. He noticed Solo in the back, looking directly at him. Remembering his previous run-ins with Solo in vivid detail—the ride on the front of the car and Solo getting tangled up in the bell-pulls at the church—the vicar said a quick prayer under his breath and pulled on the brakes of his bike in order to give Solo's car plenty of room. He wasn't going to, as he put it, "take any chances with that dog". The vicar had always thought Solo was a danger to humanity and had vowed to avoid him at all costs from now on.

Unfortunately, due to the heavy rain, the bike's tires started to skid. Panicking slightly, the vicar tried to steer the bike to safety and away from the hedges that lined the side of the lane. In doing so, he steered too hard and too fast, causing the front wheel of the bike to hit a deep puddle, slowing the bike dramatically. The bike came to a complete stop in the large puddle, and ever so slowly, the bike and vicar toppled over, throwing the vicar onto the muddy verge of the lane.

He sat up, rain now pouring down his neck, somewhat pleased with himself that his yellow rain gear had protected him from the worst of the water. Just then, a white delivery van sped by, its wheels hitting the puddle with full force, throwing gallons of muddy water directly onto the vicar and into his face. The van sped on, blissfully unaware of the soaking wet vicar in its wake.

The vicar looked up, his face now stained with mud and water. He was just in time to see Solo's car disappearing over a hill in the distance. He could still make out Solo, looking directly at him with a rather perplexed look on his face. The vicar, shaking water from his person, stood up, grabbed his bike, and set off, determined more than ever that he was going to avoid Solo at all costs.

As they sped away, Solo wondered, not for the first time, how it was that the vicar was always getting himself into trouble. He seemed like such a sensible person too, for a human. As Mum, Dad, and Solo continued on their way, the weather became even worse. So much so, that by the time they came to the next town and the polling station inside the local church, the streets were starting to fill with water.

"Come on," said Dad to his wife, "let's get this over with." He spoke to Solo in the back of the car. "Solo, we will be right back." And with that, Mum and Dad ran as fast as they could through the rain and into the church.

Solo watched them go, wondering not for the first time why it was humans didn't like being in the rain. Solo loved running around in the rain. He loved splashing through puddles, then, when his fur was drenched, shaking as hard as he could to get rid of the water, preferably next to a human. Their reactions were priceless.

The other thing Solo wondered was why Mum and Dad were running into the little church in the first place. Solo had some experiences with churches recently, but never had he seen Mum and Dad so eager to run into one. He pondered this situation for a moment, and then, as often happens with Solo, curiosity got the better of him.

Solo was a very observant dog, and he had noticed several things when Mum and Dad left in such a hurry. Firstly, Dad had failed to lock the car. Secondly, Mum, in a hurry to avoid getting too wet, had failed to latch her door correctly. Solo squeezed himself out from the cargo area into the passenger seats, and then onto the front seats. From there, he pushed against Mum's door, and sure enough, it swung open.

Looking around to make sure Mum and Dad weren't on their way back, Solo ran across the small car park and into the church hall. No one saw him. The room was virtually empty. Many voters had decided to stay home, hoping that the rain would ease up a bit.

Solo noticed Mum and Dad, each head-down in a separate little cubicle, looking at some kind of screen. They were so focused on their activities that they didn't pay attention to him. Neither did the two volunteers who were running the polling station. The complete lack of voters meant both volunteers decided it was time for a cup of tea, so they had gone to the small kitchen in the back of the hall to brew up the kettle.

This meant Solo was free to wander. Each voting booth was about six feet tall with sides to protect whatever the voter was doing from prying eyes. He looked up at the terminal, which voters were to use to cast their ballot. Solo couldn't see what was on the screen from his height, but he could make out the glow coming from the screen.

Determined to see what Mum and Dad were so diligently staring at, he jumped up, resting his front paws on the screen. He stared at all the pretty lights, quite fascinated by what he was looking at. Next to the screen were a series of buttons, but it was the large, red one that caught his attention the most. Solo sniffed at it, then, quite accidentally, pushed it with his nose.

The machine made a slight click, then a beep. The screen then changed from a white to blue color. The machine beeped one more time, and then fell silent. Solo stared at it for a few moments more, but nothing happened.

Bored, he let his front legs fall back to the ground. Still not understanding why Mum and Dad were still staring at their screens—after all, nothing much had happened when Solo did the same—he made his way back outside and jumped into the still open door of the family SUV. He decided he much preferred being on the front passenger seat, so he rested there on his haunches, looking at the rain, but not before giving one almighty shake to remove as much water as possible, showering the inside of the car with water and not a little amount of damp, dog hair.

This was how Mum and Dad found Solo a few minutes later: sitting comfortably in the front passenger seat, water dripping slowly from the ceiling, mingled with the odd, fluffy ball of dog hair. The front seat was so wet from where Solo had been sitting that Mum had to ride in the back seat for the journey home.

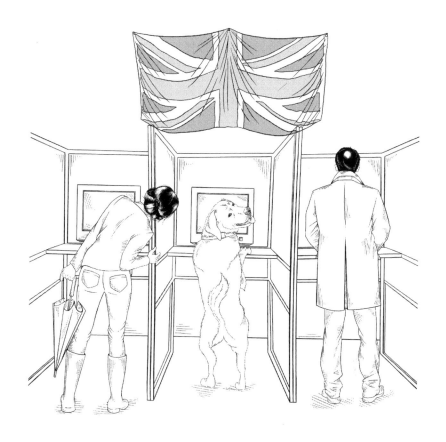

Mum and Dad never did figure out how the front door of the car was opened, nor how it was that Solo got so wet. Needless to say, Dad vowed to soon purchase a dog guard for the back of the SUV, designed to prevent Solo from jumping out from the cargo area and into the passenger area. For the short drive home, Solo lay down on his blanket in the back of the car and allowed the motion of the car to rock him gently to sleep.

That evening, Dad stayed up late to watch the election results roll in. Solo decided to keep him company in the living room, lying on the floor in front of Dad, one eye open on the television, the other half-closed as he struggled to stay awake. The sound of heavy rain still pattered against the windows. Solo still couldn't understand what it was that Dad found so compelling about elections; it seemed extremely boring to him.

Just then, Dad called out to his wife to come in and watch with him. It seemed the reporters on the television were about to call the election results for the area that Solo's family lived. As Mum sat down next to Dad, Solo decided to pay attention. If his family was paying attention to this, then clearly Solo needed to pay attention as well.

The man on the television read out the results. Suddenly there was a gasp in the audience on television, and Mum and Dad gasped too. It seemed that the person Dad had wanted to win the election in their area had lost by a single vote.

"One vote! One vote!" said Dad loudly to the television. "Our man lost by one vote! When does that ever happen? Never!" he yelled again as he answered his own question. "I would love to know who that one voter was," Dad continued. "He needs to be run out of town." Dad sat back in the chair with a big thud, thoroughly upset by the election result.

Solo watched Dad's outburst from the floor just in front of the TV. If Dad was upset, then that meant Solo was upset too. Who was this person that had allowed Dad's "man" to lose by a single vote? Solo decided he would like to know too.

6. Solo and the Mayor

Dad was upset. Recently there had been a general election, and the MP who won was the MP Dad *didn't* want to win. Dad had voted for his opponent. To make matters worse, Dad's choice for MP had lost by *one* vote. Even a week after the election, Dad could not get over this loss.

Every morning at breakfast as Dad read the paper and the kids had their breakfast, he would complain bitterly about how his idea of the perfect politician had lost by one vote. "One vote!" said Dad for the hundredth time. "We lost by one vote. I still cannot believe it."

The children had learned by now to ignore Dad's tirades on this subject. Instead, they kept their heads down as they read comics and ate their cereal.

It was Mum's job to soothe Dad. "Calm down, dear," she said. "You're going to give yourself a heart attack."

Dad simply said, "Harrumph," and went back to hiding behind his newspaper.

As usual, Solo was listening intently to the conversation from his bed under the kitchen table. The fact that Solo had inadvertently voted for the eventual winner of the election never occurred to him.

Solo tried, though he often failed, to ignore what was going on with his family. So long as he could take a nap in the afternoon sun, chase a squirrel every now and then, and get an occasional tummy rub, he was happy. But every once in a while, Solo felt compelled to see if he could help out his family. The fact that his attempts at helping often ended in disaster was immaterial. He loved his family, and if he felt he could help, he would.

It bothered Solo that Dad seemed to be upset about something. So when Dad got up to go and catch his train, Solo followed him to the door, and rubbed his large head against Dad's knee. Dad stroked Solo's head.

"I can always count on you, can't I, boy?" Dad said, forgetting how many moments of embarrassment Solo had caused his family. "You'd never vote for that guy."

Solo nodded in agreement and stuck out a paw for Dad to shake. Then he watched as Dad drove off, determined to help improve Dad's mood.

Back in the house, Solo temporarily forgot about his promise to help Dad. It was a nice day and, having eaten a hearty breakfast, Solo's next plan was to take a nap by the back door and let the early morning sun warm him up. Solo liked being by the back door. He could lie on the cool grass, sun on his back, and listen out for any activities going on just inside the kitchen. He padded over to his favorite spot, did his usual circle of the area, lay down and closed his eyes.

He awoke to the sound of Mum talking on the telephone. She sounded quite excited.

"Well, I never," she said. And, "Are you sure? It sounds very exciting. I need to check with my husband."

Solo lifted up his majestic head so he could listen better. Whoever it was that Mum was talking to had got her animated about something. Whatever it was, Solo wanted to be in on the action. So he stood up and did a quick stretch, which consisted of pushing out his front legs, keeping his head close to the ground, and raising his rear as far as it would go.

Having accomplished this piece of exercise for the day, Solo walked into the kitchen in an attempt to find out what all the fuss was about. He found Mum sitting at the kitchen table, the phone still in her hand, staring off into space, clearly still thinking about the recent phone call.

Seeing Solo, she said, "Guess what, Solo? I'm going to be mayor."

Solo didn't know what that meant, but if Mum was excited about being mayor, then Solo was excited too. Mum put the phone down, thought for a second, and then picked it up and dialed Dad. Solo listened as she explained to Dad how a friend of hers was recommending she run for mayor, and that she was probably going to do so. Solo could just make out Dad's voice on the phone, seemingly encouraging his wife to run.

That night, the entire family—Mum, Dad, and the children—sat around the kitchen table, excitedly discussing what needed to be done. It turned out the old mayor was retiring, and it was expected that only Mum and one other person would run for the office. While being mayor of the family's small village was unpaid, it did come with prestige and some power over how the village was run. The family agreed that Mum was the best person for the job.

A few days later, Mum's opponent was announced: a retired army officer who was simply known as "The Captain", a woman with whom Mum'd had problems in the past. She'd been the bake-sale organizer who tried unsuccessfully to humiliate Mum. Now, Mum had no doubt that The Captain's reason for running was simply because she couldn't stand the idea of Mum winning.

The election was only thirty days away, and soon both sides were putting up posters and putting leaflets on people's doors explaining why Mum or The Captain should be mayor. The village was small, so it didn't take long for the family to go door to door campaigning for Mum, often with Solo in tow. Solo enjoyed going door to door as the homeowners spent more time making a fuss over him than speaking to Mum about the issues.

Two days before the election, Mum presented her case to the residents at the village hall. Standing on the small stage for over an hour, she found the whole process quite exhausting, especially as she also had to answer questions. Finally, at the end of her time, she invited her entire family, including Solo, onto the stage so that the voters could get to know Mum better.

As they stood there introducing themselves, a tennis ball that Dad had kept to amuse Solo should he become bored fell out of his pocket. Naturally, Solo spotted this immediately and scampered after the ball, much to the amusement of the assembled audience. The crowd even gave a round of applause when Solo caught the rolling ball and proudly, head and tail held high, came back to the center of the stage, rolled on his back and started to chew contentedly.

The next day Solo, yet again, was on the front page of the local newspaper, as a reporter had caught the moment on camera.

"Unbelievable," said Mum at breakfast. "My big moment, and what happens? No picture of me, just a picture of Solo on his back, chewing a tennis ball. They didn't even mention what a great speech I gave. It's all Solo."

"Well you know what newspapers are like," said her husband, attempting to support his wife. "Anything for a headline."

"Yes, just look at that headline," said Mum. She picked up the newspaper and read aloud, "'Solo for Mayor', it says. And look at the caption underneath his picture. 'Solo, the dog that rescued the local church, proves that he is qualified to be mayor by showing how to have some fun.' How embarrassing. My own dog makes the front page of the newspaper and I didn't." Mum stared into her cup of morning tea.

"Well as I said," said her husband, "you know what newspapers are like. Anything for a laugh. Besides, the voters know Solo is *your* dog, and they know how he is, and that reflects on you."

"I know," sighed his wife. "That's what worries me."

"In a positive way, dear," said her husband. "In a positive way."

Solo, who had been listening intently from his bed in the kitchen, wasn't the least bit interested in the conversation. He had just had a nice breakfast and was chewing yet again on the same tennis ball he had gone after the night before.

Voting was the next day and the family was out bright and early at the polling station, set up this time in the church that Solo had so famously rescued a few months earlier. The front of the church was now ensconced in scaffolding, as the church made good use of the money Solo had raised to rescue the bell tower.

While the children were too young to vote, they had accompanied their parents as a show of support. As they were walking in, the same photographer who had taken Solo's picture the night before took one of the family. He came over and shook Solo's paw.

"You must be very proud of Solo," the reporter said to Mum. "Rescuing the church and all that."

"Yes, very," said Mum stiffly as the family kept going into the church. She was still upset that the newspaper put Solo's picture on the front page and not hers.

Inside the church, a small table had been set up to vote. This being a very small election, old-fashioned paper ballots were used. The ballot was very simple. It read, "For Mayor, I choose," and then Mum's name and The Captain's name appeared underneath. Opposite each name was a box, in which voters were required to place a large X depending on who they were voting for.

As Mum and Dad registered to vote, Solo and the children wandered around the old church. Towards the back of the church, Solo ran head-first into the young vicar. This was the same vicar that Solo—through no fault of his own, he would claim—had embarrassed or minorly injured on numerous occasions.

Ever since he had met Solo, the Vicar had made it his life's work to stay as far away from Solo as possible. This was because, often, no good came from being in the vicinity of "that dog". Although, the vicar would admit to himself, usually when he was feeling more generous, that Solo had indeed been the main reason the church had raised enough money to save the old tower in the first place.

Still, a nervous tingle would go down the vicar's spine if he came close to Solo. And here he was, "that dog", loose and seemingly unsupervised in *his* church. As Solo trotted quickly up the aisle towards the voting table, the vicar felt another shudder go down his spine.

Solo, seeing the vicar disappear up the aisle and sensing a game, ran after him. The vicar, not realizing Solo was after him, slowed down right by the table where Mum and Dad were placing their Xs on the ballot papers.

Solo, now running full tilt, tried to stop on the slippery, hard, stone surface, but failed to stop before barreling into the vicar, pushing him into the table, and sending both the vicar and the table tumbling. As if right on cue, the reporter showed up with his camera and snapped a few pictures of the vicar, laying on the floor as ballot papers fell like snow around him.

Mum and Dad helped the vicar up, picked up all the unused ballot papers and placed them on the righted table. The vicar smoothed his ruffled hair, gave Solo a look that would wilt a flower, and strode out of the church door with as much dignity as he could muster.

That night Mum could hardly sleep, as she was so excited at the possibility of being elected mayor that every five minutes she would prod her husband, saying, "This is going to be so great. Imagine it: me, the mayor."

Her husband grunted something unintelligible and rolled over, trying to go back to sleep and thinking he would be really happy when his wife lost some of her election fever.

The next day, the family waited anxiously for the local newspaper to be delivered, as it would be covering the election results. Suddenly the letterbox opened and the unmissable sound of several papers landing on the tiled hallway permeated the house.

"They're here!" Mum shrieked, and she jumped out of her chair and ran excitedly to the front door. For a moment, there was complete silence as Dad and the kids crossed their fingers. Suddenly there was another shriek, this time not in a good way.

Dad cringed. "I think Mum lost," he whispered to his children. "Remember: be supportive." He looked up as his wife came back into the kitchen. "How was it?" he asked her.

She threw the paper down on the table, front page up. There in big bold letters was the headline. It read, "BIG UPSET: SOLO THE DOG ELECTED MAYOR".

"What on earth?" said Dad. "Let me see that." He picked the paper up and read aloud.

"'Solo the Dog has been elected Mayor when more voters wrote his name on the ballot papers than voted for either of the listed candidates. This newspaper intends to reach out to Solo for comment.'"

Mum held her head in her hands. "Oh, the embarrassment," she moaned. "Beaten in an election, not by my opposition, but by my *own* dog! How will I ever live this down?" She rested her head on the kitchen table and rolled from side to side.

The children looked at the paper closely, for underneath a picture of Solo was another picture. This one showed the vicar, flat on his back, with hundreds of paper ballots falling around him. The caption under that picture read, "Vicar upsets the vote."

It wasn't long before yet another picture of Solo was on the front page of the newspaper. This time it showed a beaming Solo, sitting on his haunches, with the mayor's chain, glistening gold, around his neck. Standing beside Solo was the outgoing mayor, a huge grin on his face. Standing next to the mayor was a very glum looking Mum. And standing the other side of Solo was an even more glum looking vicar. The headline read, "MAYOR SOLO PROMISES FREE HUGS".

"Oh good grief," said Mum as she read the headline. "I think it's time we moved."

Solo, realizing Mum was disappointed about something, came over and rested his head on her knee. Looking her in the eye, he seemed to wink at Mum.

Mum reached over and rubbed his large, white head. "Oh, Solo," she said, "whatever are we going to do with you?"

Solo thought for a moment and decided he had absolutely no idea.

7. Solo and the Snow Day

Snow was just one thing in a long list that made Solo very happy indeed. The list also included the following: ice cream, long walks, long naps, chasing squirrels, chewing on tennis balls, eating, and generally hanging out with his family.

The problem with snow, however, was that Solo never really knew when or even if it was going to happen. Solo could always count on having a tennis ball to chew or finding a squirrel to annoy, but snow was different. It was a rare event. And even if it did snow, often it wasn't around long enough to really enjoy. It either snowed just enough to make the landscape all white and picturesque, but not enough to play in. Or there might be a wonderful, deep layer of snow only for the temperature to warm the next day and turn the snow to a mushy goo of slush.

Then one day it finally happened. Slowly at first, a light layer of sleet covered the landscape. This did not in itself promise true fun for Solo. Then, overnight, a heavy snowstorm hit, forcing roads to close, schools to be shut down, and dogs and children to become animated in their excitement.

Solo looked out the glass back door of the family's home at an amazing wonderland. Deep snow covered everything. Tree branches bent under the extra weight. The long, deep lawn that overlooked a picturesque valley seemed to blend into the distant landscape that was now all one color. Even though it had stopped snowing, every now and then, a gust of wind would whip up some snow and move it from one part of the back garden to another.

The children were beside themselves with excitement. Schools were closed for what adults called a "snow day", which meant all the time in the world for the kids to go and play in the white stuff. Suitably dressed in extra-warm clothing, the children couldn't wait to get outside. Solo, quite naturally, wanted to follow.

Often, where the kids went, he went. Unless they were playing dress up, in which case he might be forced to wear a pink tutu and a red crown. In those situations, he tried to avoid detection. Not in the case of snow though.

They were going to play in the snow, so Solo was going to play in the snow. He was just about to follow the kids outside when a determined hand pulled on his collar and reined him in.

"Not so fast, Solo," said Mum. "First we need to put these on your paws." One by one, she placed some very colorful, old socks on each of Solo's paws. "We don't want you getting frostbite, Solo," said Mum. And with that, she opened the door to let Solo out.

Solo looked at his feet. Each was covered in a colored sock. One was red, one was blue with pink, and the other two were bright orange. "How humiliating," thought Solo. He hoped that Sunny, his poodle friend next door, wouldn't see how he was dressed, as he knew he would never live it down. Solo vowed to take the socks off once he was out of Mum's view. Wearing these was almost as bad as having to wear a pink tutu.

Outside in the deep snow, Solo tried to run after the children, but as big as Solo was, the snow was deeper. He found it very hard to move. He quickly discovered the best way to get from one part of the garden to another was to use his brute strength to plow ahead. Soon Solo was deep in the snow, his white body blending in, pushing forward like a submarine just below the surface of the ocean.

Solo found this whole thing exhausting, but also exhilarating. Then he discovered an even easier way to get around in the deep snow; he would leap from spot to spot, like a mountain goat jumping from rock to rock. This was great fun and, sure enough, he eventually made his way to where the children were playing. But just as he got there, the children ran towards the front of the house, where they had decided to make a snowman that could be seen by passersby on the road.

Eventually, an exhausted Solo made his way to the front, where the construction of a snowman was already well underway. Solo lay down in order to catch his breath and watch. The children had been joined by several other neighborhood kids, and soon half a dozen children were actively building snowmen and snow forts or having great snowball battles.

Solo decided to stay well away, as he knew before long he would become a target of snowballs or even seconded as some kind of snowy white, animal weapon. Solo was quite content to keep his distance from the melee and sit by the snow-covered driveway, observing from a safe distance. Solo soon became bored and started to paw at the snow in an attempt to dig a hole, but he found the socks on his feet were impeding his progress. He attempted to remove one of them by pulling at it with his teeth, but he had no luck.

He was just about to try again, when he glanced up and noticed a small figure standing on the other side of the road. The figure was dressed in a giant winter coat that seemed about five sizes too big. A stretched-on bobble hat covered the head, and large, green Wellington boots were on the feet. Every item of clothing looked either too big or too small.

Solo stopped and looked closer. He could see that under that giant coat was a little girl, and when he looked closer, he could see a little boy peeping out every now and then from around the girl's shoulders. They didn't move. They simply stared at the children in the front garden who were yelling, screaming, wrestling in the snow, and generally having the time of their lives.

Solo looked at them for a few moments, wondering why they didn't come over to play with the other children. In his experience, if kids saw other kids having fun, most of the time they didn't need any encouragement whatsoever to go and play. This difference in behavior piqued Solo's curiosity. And when Solo is curious about something, it doesn't take much incentive for Solo to investigate.

Solo wandered across the unplowed, snow-covered road to the children who stared, mouths open, as this giant of a dog got closer. Solo could tell they weren't sure how friendly he would be. So Solo stopped in the middle of the road and gave them one of his biggest smiles.

The children relaxed, the little girl saying very quietly to the little boy, "He seems friendly."

Slowly, Solo walked right up to them and nuzzled the little girl very gently. The little boy, sensing Solo was indeed a very friendly dog, came out from behind the little girl and rubbed Solo's giant head. Solo nuzzled him too. Unfortunately, the little boy was not ready, and Solo, forgetting his own strength for a moment, knocked the boy down in the snow. Feeling guilty, Solo bent down and, grabbing the boy by the collar of his coat in his mouth, lifted him gently to his feet.

Just then, the noise across the street from all the children playing in the snow reached a crescendo as one side in the giant snowball fight seemed to have gained victory. The little boy and girl turned their attention from Solo and looked longingly across the road. Solo now understood what was happening. The boy and girl wanted to play with Solo's family and their friends but were too shy to go over and to ask if they could join in.

Solo decided there and then that it would now be his mission to make this happen. And as we know, once Solo makes his mind up about something, he has a tendency to follow through with it.

Solo tried to nudge the little girl across the road, but she refused, the little boy once again hiding behind the her. Solo tried pushing both of them this time. And still they refused to move. Solo got an idea. He lay down on his belly, hoping that the children would get the message.

At first the little girl didn't understand, but then she said, "I think he wants us to ride him," to the little boy. They both gently got onto Solo's broad back.

"Oof," thought Solo as they both sat on his back and grabbed his fur tightly. He had meant just the little boy getting on, not the boy *and* the girl.

Solo was lying in the snow, now with two small children on his back. How would he get up? Solo pushed with his front legs so he was almost in a sitting position. Both children immediately fell back into the snow. As they were grabbing onto his fur, it felt to Solo like they had taken all the fur off his back with them.

Laughing now, the children tried to get back on, but Solo had other ideas. He lay down and, once the girl had helped the little boy onto his back, stood up immediately, preventing the girl from getting on. She figured out Solo's physical needs from that and took her brother's hand, walking beside Solo.

Solo walked carefully across the road, keeping pace with the little girl, his paws slightly deeper in the snow from the weight of his tiny passenger. Although he couldn't see their faces, Solo could hear the children's giggles.

It was not a pain-free experience for Solo as the little boy gripped hard on his fur to make sure he wouldn't fall off. But Solo was determined to see his mission through.

Eventually, the trio made it to the front of Solo's house, where the snowball fight had started up again. Distracted as the children were by the fight, no one noticed Solo and the new children until he was right in the middle of the battle between the two sides. All snowball throwing ceased immediately as the group of children stopped, snowballs still in hand, to watch Solo, with the boy still on his back, trudge slowly to a halt.

Solo's passenger and the passenger's sister were unsure what to do next, so Solo, in an effort to move things along, simply sat down, and the boy slid unceremoniously off his back and into the snow. The little girl helped her brother stand up and brush the snow off. No one said a word.

Solo, fed up with the lack of action, and the thought that all his efforts might go for naught, went over to his own family's children, and roughly pushed the daughter towards the new arrivals. "Now that ought to do it," thought Solo.

The daughter stared at the new arrivals for a second, and then said, "What's your name?" to the little girl.

Very softly, the little girl said her name and that of her brother. Once the ice was broken, the new arrivals were invited to play with the other children. It seemed the boy and girl had only just arrived in the village and had yet to make any friends. When they heard all the happy voices coming from Solo's house they had decided to investigate.

For the rest of the day, the boy and girl played with the other children, until it was decided that rather than make another snowman, they should all help make a snow-throne and play "Kings and Queens". After some effort, a throne of sorts was built, but who should sit in first?

After a few minutes of debate, the little girl pointed at Solo. "He should sit in it," she said in her now full voice, having found her confidence among her new friends. It was agreed by all. Solo would sit on the throne.

Solo needed no encouragement. He allowed himself to be led over to the snow-throne, and sat down, a huge grin on his face. Thinking quickly, the little girl made a crown out of some branches and leaves she had pulled from a small bush. She pushed the crown down hard on Solo's head.

Solo winced slightly as she had forgotten to remove any thorns that were hidden in the crown. Still, this was a small price to pay, he thought, knowing he had helped some children find a circle of new friends. Besides, he was now king. Something he knew he was always destined to be. Even if it was only for a little while.

8. Solo's Second Christmas

Solo's second Christmas with his family was coming up fast. After being adopted from the animal shelter, Solo had quickly settled into the family's routine, but one thing he couldn't get enough of was Christmas. He had been disappointed to learn that Christmas only took place once a year. As far as Solo was concerned, just like the kids in the family, Christmas should take place every single day.

When the family tree had been put up and decorated in the living room, Solo began to get very excited. There weren't any presents under the tree yet—it was far too early for that—but Solo certainly was starting to feel that the Christmas spirit in the air. The weather had turned much colder, the nights were much longer, and the village was lit up far and wide by Christmas lights.

He particularly liked the idea of going to the village hall again to see if he could understand what a Christmas play was all about, because last year he hadn't been allowed in. This year though, Mum and Dad had decided that Solo wasn't even going to have wait outside the village hall like last time. Given the results of Solo's last visit, even though the resulting catastrophe was not proven to be Solo's fault, Dad in particular had felt it best to leave Solo behind.

It was Dad who suspected Solo had somehow been involved when the trap door on the stage had opened and one of the stars of the show fell through. Even though he couldn't prove it, finding the star's ballet slipper next to Solo had only toughened Dad's attitude about Solo attending another play.

But the latest play was a week away, and Solo was far more excited about something new. Christmas caroling. Last year he had heard a few singers come to the doors to sing carols, but he hadn't paid too much attention to them. This year, he learned by listening in to his family's conversations as he lay under the large kitchen table, that his family had decided to actually *go* Christmas caroling around the village.

Solo was not sure what that meant, but from what he gathered, his family was to go as a group from house to house, singing carols, and holding some lanterns with candles in them as they went. The plan was to raise money for the village hall which was in dire need of a new roof. In fact, this year's play may not happen if there was a sudden burst of heavy rain. The roof was that bad. Some emergency repairs had been planned, but even that would cost money. So Mum, Dad and the kids would do their part to raise some ready cash.

Solo had gone door to door around the village in the past. Once to help Mum get elected mayor. The fact that Solo had become mayor instead was just a minor hiccup. Naturally, Solo expected his family to take him door to door once more, this time to go Christmas caroling. His ears pricked up when he heard his name become part of the conversation.

"So," said Mum, "do we dare take Solo caroling with us?"

There was a pause, as the weight of the question sunk in. The kids were, of course, all for Solo joining them. But then again, they weren't the ones who had to clean up Solo's little catastrophes.

Dad thought for a moment, then said, "Well the walk will do him good. And we can put some of those joke reindeer antlers on him."

"Are you sure?" said Mum. She loved Solo as much as Dad, but it was Dad who often ended up on the wrong side of Solo's little escapades.

"Sure, why not?" said Dad. "I'll make sure to keep his lead tight. How much trouble could he cause?" A question no member of the family dared to answer. Dad looked under the table and spoke to Solo. "Wanna come Christmas caroling, Solo? Of course you do."

Solo looked back at Dad. Whatever this Christmas caroling thing was, if his family was doing it, then Solo was all in.

Soon enough the evening of the caroling arrived. Mum had purchased a bright red lead for Solo, and as promised, he was now fitted with a pair of fake reindeer antlers which went over his head. For extra fun, they also lit up and flashed their lights. As a final touch, Mum had outfitted Solo with a small reindeer bell attached to his collar. Solo loved all of his new trappings.

To add to the holiday cheer, Mum had arranged for some Christmas lanterns to be hung from short poles which the children would carry. Mum would carry a bag for the donations as well as some papers with the lyrics for the carols. But Dad had only one mission: being in charge of Solo.

The family set off in good spirits. It was very dark as the moon was hidden by clouds, but it wasn't too cold, and the family dressed accordingly. Solo of course had his own fur coat. He very much liked having the little bell, the red lead, and the reindeer antlers. It helped make Solo the center of attention at every house they visited. Solo enjoyed being the center of attention.

After a few houses, the family were getting their voices warmed up. At first they were slightly out of tune, but soon they were in their stride. Dad was a very good singer indeed, much to the embarrassment of the children. Dad would forget he was on a quiet street somewhere in a small village and would belt out the carols at the top of his lungs. The rest of Dad's family had absolutely no doubt that the entire village could hear.

They needn't go anywhere else, the children told Mum in an embarrassed whisper; all Dad needed to do was stand on the village green and everyone could hear him whether they wanted to or not.

Mum told Dad to "reign it in a little".

Dad, slightly upset that his family didn't enjoy his vocal skills, promised to do so at the next stop.

Soon they were close to the village green itself, the street lights reflecting off the tranquil pond. As it was mostly small shops next to the green, they kept walking to the next set of houses.

Solo was thoroughly enjoying himself. Even though he had felt the urge to sing along with his family, he was so caught up in the atmosphere of Christmas, the lights hanging from the houses, the decorated trees in people's homes, that he didn't feel the need to help his family out. Not like the time at the school concert. Besides, Dad was quite capable of singing for all of them.

As they walked down the street, they passed the large Christmas tree that was erected once a year in the center of the village. Standing about thirty feet tall, it lit up the surrounding area, including the old, stone, war memorial, which still had some flowers of remembrance on it. The family paused for a moment to take in the contrasts of a memorial and the light of the tree right next to the village green.

Solo thought it all wonderful, then realized he needed to relieve himself, and as they were close to the green, what better place to do it? He pulled at the lead, encouraging Dad to walk towards the green.

"No, Solo," Dad said, "we're going this way." But Solo refused to move. "Solo, come on!" said Dad. Solo stood stock still.

"I think he's telling you he needs to go to the bathroom," said his wife.

"Oh, sorry, Solo. Yes, you're probably right," Dad said to his wife. "Come on, boy. I'm sorry. I wasn't paying attention. I suppose you're like us, right? When you gotta go, you gotta go. I'll take him over to the green, let him sniff around for a bit. We'll catch up," he told his family.

They were secretly relieved. It meant, for at least a few minutes, they could sing some carols without having Dad bellow out a song at hundreds of decibels.

Dad led Solo over to a part of the village green that was not too far from the Christmas tree. The light from the tree lit up the whole area, so Dad let Solo off the lead. Solo, pleased to be off the lead, wandered around the green looking for a good place to do his business, but first he decided he was thirsty and went over to the edge of the pond, where he took a large drink of water.

Adding all that extra weight to his stomach made going to the bathroom an imperative. So he smelled around for a suitable location. Going closer to the large Christmas tree, he decided on the spot. He paused for a second. Then, having finished, he smelled around a bit more just in case he had missed anything interesting.

But Dad was calling. "Come on, Solo, time to go."

Reluctantly, Solo stopped sniffing and walked over to Dad, but as he did so, his sensitive nose picked up the slight smell of something burning. He stopped and looked back. Smelling it stronger this time, he turned to go and investigate, but Dad told him, "Come on Solo." Solo turned back towards Dad, but the smell was getting stronger still. He turned around once more. Now, in the light of the tree, he could see smoke coming from the area where he had gone to the bathroom.

"That's weird," he thought. "I've never seen *that* before."

Dad was about to yell at Solo to hurry up when he caught sight of what Solo was looking at. Coming out of the ground where Solo had just been was a set of flames. Small at first, but getting larger by the second. He ran over to grab Solo and placed him on the lead. Then, slowly, he got closer to the scene of the fire.

Dad could see the fire was coming from an electrical box set up to power the tree and all its lights. Dad didn't want to believe it, but he did wonder if Solo had peed on it and shorted it out. Feeling a little guilty, Dad pulled Solo away from the area. Solo wasn't aware what he had done either, but he was pretty sure that he had come close to that thing on the ground and, in the interest of self-preservation, felt it best to get as far away as possible from the scene of the crime lest he somehow become connected to this ensuing catastrophe.

As they looked on, the fire spread up the wire towards the tree, like a slow-moving fuse. Dad, afraid to let Solo go so he could try and put the fire out, stared for a few seconds, his mouth open. It wasn't until the flames from the wire hit the tree and flames began to shoot into the sky that Dad found his voice. "Fire! Fire!" he yelled and pulled Solo further away from the flames.

Solo didn't need any help moving away. Like all animals, he was wary of fire. But he couldn't help wonder as they moved to a safe distance if he was somehow responsible. "How can I be," he thought? "All I did was go number one. Is my pee flammable?"

Finally, remembering he had a cell phone, Dad pulled it out and called the emergency services. As he did so, the tree became engulfed in fire, then all the lights went out. The lack of lights was more than made up for by the ever-increasing fire.

The commotion slowly drew people from their homes. Luckily, all that was burning was the tree. As Mum and the kids joined Dad to watch the fireman extinguish the flames, they asked Dad what happened.

He explained that he was simply waiting for Solo to go to the bathroom when he noticed flames coming from near where Solo had been. As he said it, the entire family looked at Solo. "Nah," said Dad. "Even Solo couldn't burn down an entire tree. Could he?" he asked plaintively.

Solo looked up at them as if to say, "You know I think I've had enough of this caroling thing. Can we go home now?"

Not daring to contemplate how Solo could have even been remotely involved, the family turned back to watch the remains of the tree as it turned to ash. Dad would spend the next few days trying to come up with ways that Solo was involved, but then decided, like so many things to do with Solo, it was best not to inquire too hard.

Finally, as the family turned to leave, they came face to face with the old war memorial which was inscribed with names of the men from the village who had died in battle. Dad paused for a moment, looking directly at the names, and with the flames from tree reflecting off the old stonework, he thought how lucky he was before leading Solo away into the night.

9. Solo and the Raft

Not too far from Solo's family's home, was a large stream which ran from the countryside, through the village, and out the other side. Over the stream on the way to the center of the village was a stone bridge, which was so old and narrow that only one car at a time could pass over it. If a car was coming in the opposite direction, one of the cars had to wait before they could cross.

It was near this old bridge that the village children would often play by the stream. They would race small boats to see which one would make it first into town. The finish line being the old dam, over which the boats would fall to their doom.

Another favorite game for the kids was to see who could skip stones the furthest. Once, the children had made a dam out of mounds of clay and dirt, which was so successful that the local council had to send workers along to dismantle it with pickaxes and shovels after it flooded a farmer's field further upstream. The kids had felt it best to stay away from the stream for a few weeks after that.

Solo would sometimes come down with the kids to watch them play, and every once in a while, swim across the stream to the other side just so he could shake all the water out of his coat and make the children wetter than they already were.

One particularly hot day, a few of the local children were trying to decide what to do when one of them suggested they go and play boats again in the stream. But the novelty of this had worn thin as the hot summer days dragged on. What the younger members of the population were in need of was a new sense of purpose, a new mission to invigorate them before they all had to return to that dreaded grown-up invention known as "school".

Then one of the girls had an idea. "I know," she said. "Let's make rafts that we can ride on, girls against boys. I bet we win too," she added emphatically as she blew a particularly large bubble with her gum, which then burst all over her nose.

The boys in the group laughed derisively at this notion, that mere *girls* could beat *boys* at anything. So the challenge was offered and taken. It was agreed the group would meet the next day with their rafts, one for the girl team, and one for the boy team.

As Solo's family included a boy and a girl, the siblings would be competing with each other. And as Solo loved both of the children equally, he decided he couldn't pick a side. He would simply follow along from the bank of the stream, barking his encouragement at both sides of this epic duel.

So the children broke into their respective groups. Base camp for constructing the boys raft was at a friend's house, while the girls were using Solo's house. Normally Solo wouldn't go within fifty feet of a group of girls consisting of the daughter and her friends as there was a sizable risk he would be seconded to dress up in a pink tutu or be forced to drink a cup of pretend tea. But this was different. The girls were determined to beat the boys in not only winning the race down the stream, but to also show the boys that girls are quite capable of making a great raft.

As the girls scrounged for planks of wood and rope to build their raft, Solo lay down to observe the proceedings. Although, just to be sure, he kept a safe distance in case the novelty of building a raft faded and the girls returned to games of tea parties and pink tutus for Solo.

The next day, the kids congregated alongside the stream just below the old bridge, boys on one side of the stream, the girls on the other. The boys had included a pirate flag, and the head of a Halloween dragon that had seen better days. Both had been affixed to the front of their craft. The girls raft included a large mast which went up about four feet. Attached to the mast was a large sail made from an old sheet.

Once the boys saw this, an intense argument ensued. The boys claimed this was cheating as the wind might help push the girls raft along. The girls pointed out there wasn't any wind, so it wouldn't make a difference anyway. The boys said this was not the point. Just because there was not any wind now didn't mean there wouldn't be later.

This arguing went on for a few minutes until both sides became exhausted, and they realized they were wasting time. Somewhat begrudgingly the boys agreed to let the sail issue slide, but if the wind picked up, well, that was another story.

Both teams waded into the shallow stream and climbed aboard, with one team member holding the raft back. They counted down... "Go!"

The last team member of each side climbed aboard and the rafts set sail. Unsurprisingly they were neck and neck at first. But both teams knew, not far down the stream, it narrowed so that only one raft at a time could pass through before the stream widened again. Whoever was first through the gap would have a good chance of maintaining the lead to the finish line near the village green right before the stream reached the dam.

Both teams paddled furiously, determined to make it to the gap first. Solo, running along the bank, shouted what he believed to be words of encouragement to either team. To the kids on the rafts, it simply sounded like Solo was barking a lot. As the rafts got close to the where the stream narrowed, the girls were aided by a slight gust of wind, which caught their sail and propelled them along just enough to be faster than the boys so that they made it to the gap first.

The boys howled in disbelief. The girls yelled back that the boys were simply upset they hadn't thought to build a raft with a sail. The girls stuck their tongues out at the boys as they pulled ahead.

Solo, running fast to keep up, followed the girls raft to the finish line right in the center of the village, where the stream widened and the pace of the water slowed. The girls paddled over to the bank where Solo was waiting. Pulling the raft slightly onto the bank, the out-of-breath girls jumped up and down for joy and hugged each other as they waited for the boys to arrive.

When the boys did pull up, another argument immediately ensued about the validity of having a sail on one raft and not on another. While the two sides were arguing, Solo noticed that the boys' raft had not been properly pulled up on to the bank as they were in such a hurry to accuse the girls of cheating.

As the boys and girls continued to argue, one of the smaller girls, in a moment of anger, pushed the boys' raft away. "Serves you right," she said. As she pushed the raft away, she lost her balance slightly and fell onto the raft as it floated away from the bank. Panicking slightly, she yelled, "Help!" as the raft drifted further out.

The other children stopped arguing and, realizing what had happened, chased after the raft down the bank of the stream. Some of the boys and girls jumped on the girls' raft and gave chase.

Without thinking, Solo, understanding what had happened, jumped in the stream after the little girl and the raft. Swimming with all his might, he soon caught up and noticed trailing behind the raft was the rope that was used to tie the raft to its moorings. After a few tries, he was able to grab the rope in his strong mouth and tried to pull the raft away from the middle of the stream and towards the bank.

The children on the side of the stream yelled encouragement to Solo. Meanwhile, the other children on the girls' raft were slowly catching up as Solo was able to slow down the raft by simply pulling with all his might. The girl on the raft was less frightened now, as she understood Solo was doing his best to slow the raft down and take it towards the side of the stream.

But just as Solo was starting to make some progress, the children on the side of the stream started to yell much more frantically. As the stream started to leave the village, it widened even further, and he remembered that the stream would be blocked by a dam, which the water would then flow over, as part of the complex of an old water-powered mill that was built over one-hundred years ago. The dam created a small waterfall that, should they reach it, Solo, the raft, and the little girl would go tumbling over into the swirling waters below.

Redoubling his efforts, and with the girl now yelling hysterically, Solo was able to slowly guide the raft to the side of the stream, just enough so the kids on the bank, along with some helpful grown-ups, got the girl and the raft safely to shore. A large policeman, who had been alerted to the pandemonium, waded into the stream and lifted Solo out by the scruff of his neck.

Solo lay on the ground, too out of breath to even shake the water off. He simply laid there, his big eyes even bigger, as he made sure all the kids were okay.

Over the next few days, Solo was fuss over, first by the little girl's family, and then by his. And once again, Solo made the front page of the local newspaper. This time because the mayor of the small village where Solo lived presented him with a special gold medal, which he wore with pride around his large neck. More importantly, the little girl who Solo had rescued gave him a big kiss and a brand new set of tennis balls to play with.

10. Solo's Lucky Day

Solo was in a good mood. The sun was shining, he had eaten a hearty breakfast, he had managed to annoy a squirrel or two, he had taken a turn around the back garden, and, deciding that was enough exercise for the moment, had come back into the house and plopped himself down on his bed under the kitchen table in order to take a well-deserved nap. He was just about to nod off, when he heard a slight commotion by the front door. Recognizing the voice of his friend, the mailman, Solo put off taking a nap, at least for a few moments, as he bounded towards the front door.

Sure enough, it was his friend, delivering the biggest parcel Solo had ever seen. Mum was signing for it as the mailman struggled to get it through the front door and into the hallway. Slightly out of breath from the effort, he wiped his forehead with the back of his hand and declined Mum's kind offer for a glass of water.

"I think it's something my husband ordered for his upcoming camping trip," said Mum, "although, why it's so big, I have absolutely no idea." She stared at the large box, wondering how long it would be before her husband deigned to move it from her pristine hallway.

Spying Solo, the mailman crouched down and told Solo to come on over. "Hello, Solo, how are you, boy? Still causing mischief and mayhem?" As he spoke, he rubbed Solo's head rigorously.

Solo smiled. "Now this was more like it," he thought.

"Stay away from my van though, Solo," continued his friend. "I don't want a repeat of last time." The mailman was referring to the time Solo had jumped into the back of his van and had gone for a ride without him even knowing Solo was on board. Waving goodbye to Solo and Mum, the mailman went on his way, whistling a loud, headache-causing whistle as he went.

Solo wondered, not for the first time, why he couldn't whistle as, no matter how hard he tried, all that seemed to come out of his mouth was something that sounded like a loud burp. With the parcel still leaning precariously against her beautiful wallpaper, Mum simply sighed and went back about her business, leaving Solo to ponder what could possibly be in this massive cardboard box. Solo approached the box, which toward over him, sniffing as we went.

At first all he could smell was the cardboard, but as he got closer, the faintest of familiar scents reached his highly sensitive nose. It was the smell of a tennis ball, Solo's most favorite thing in the whole, wide world. Slowly Solo moved around the base of box, sniffing intently as he went, there was no doubt in his mind now, that the entire box contained nothing but tennis balls.

What Dad would want with literally hundreds of tennis balls never once crossed Solo's mind. All he knew was that between him and nirvana was a thin layer of cardboard. Solo knew, though, that no matter how great the temptation, he could not risk chewing his way into the box despite his knowledge that this was something he was absolutely capable of doing. Once he started to chew, he knew, even if he only took one ball out, that he would be blamed for the hole, and no amount of "what, me?" expressions he might try would be able to negate his guilt.

So instead of chewing in search of one tennis ball, Solo decided to wait until Dad opened the box later that evening, and then he would do his best begging act in the hope that Dad would at least give him one. Although, as has been noted many times, Solo is not a very patient dog.

That evening Solo waited with ever increasing anticipation for Dad to come home and open the box. But Dad did not come home. It was only later in the evening, right before bed time for the family, that Solo heard Mum talking to Dad on the phone, that he realized that Dad was away on business and would not be home for at least another three days.

"Three days!" thought Solo. "How can I wait that long?" But once again, there was nothing Solo could do, so against every fiber of his being, Solo resisted temptation and went to sleep, dreaming of mountains and mountains of tennis balls.

The next day, the large brown box was still in the hallway. Mum had decided that if Dad wanted such a large, heavy box delivered, then he would be the one to move it out of her hallway, even though seeing the box there for three days might just give her headache. Like Solo, she had decided there was nothing she could do about it until Dad came home.

For Solo, however, his entire day was starting to revolve around the giant box and all those tennis balls. Deciding that the temptation was too much, he went to the garden to avoid the tennis ball smell that was permeating the entire house. He didn't understand why the smell wasn't bothering his family as they went around their usual business of school, homework, cleaning, and writing.

Unfortunately, Solo didn't find too many distractions in the back garden. Despite it being another beautiful, sunny day with an overabundance of squirrels for him to chase, Solo's mind constantly wandered back to the giant box of tennis balls. What's more, he had thoroughly convinced himself that he could smell the tennis balls all the way out in the back garden.

He decided to lie on his back and roll around. Perhaps that would help. But all that did was give his enemy, the squirrels, a reason to laugh at him from the tree above, so he soon stopped and went back inside the house.

The house was quiet. Unbeknownst to Solo, Mum had gone next door for a cup of coffee and had not felt the need to lock up or bring Solo inside. Solo was therefore alone. Alone with more temptation than any dog of Solo's temperament should have to deal with. Realizing he was on his own, Solo made his way to the hall and the giant box. Not knowing how long he would have, Solo thought through his options.

Firstly, he could do nothing, and simply wait for Dad to come home. But that wouldn't be for at least two more days. Second, he could chew on the box, just a little, to see if one single tennis ball rolled out. He could then claim innocence.

"Perhaps the box was damaged," he thought. It might have been. After all, Mum had not examined it closely. It would be completely possible for a single tennis ball to possibly, maybe, roll free by itself.

These were the two choices facing Solo: do nothing or try something. Any other dog might have decided based on past experience that "trying something" was not worth the risk. But as we know, Solo is not just any dog. Solo, after all, is Solo.

Solo continued to sniff around the lower regions of the box, looking for any sign of weakness, one that could reasonably be suggested that a tennis ball just happened to fall through. But the box was completely free of any small holes that could be exploited into a larger hole.

Pausing for a moment to decide on a course of action, Solo went through his options. If he chewed at the back of the box, the part that was leaning out and closest to the wall, his crime might not be noticed for a few days, and when it was, it was possible the hole was there all along, hidden from sight towards the wall, and simply no one had noticed.

The more Solo thought about this, the more he liked his plan. Very carefully, he stuck his head in the narrow gap between the wall and the base of the box. The space was tight, and forced Solo to try and chew on the box at an awkward angle, but he persisted. Slowly at first, he made a hole, just enough to see darkness within. Out of the hole drifted his favorite smell, the smell of glorious rubber overpowering his nose, which could only mean one thing—tennis balls.

The increased smell encouraged Solo to be more daring and to chew more. As parts of the box fell away, he started to tear at the hole. Such large amounts of cardboard came away that he had to spit them out of his mouth as they became stuck to his tongue. Soon enough, the hole was large enough for a tennis ball to fall out. In fact, it was large enough for half a dozen tennis balls to fall out. Disappointingly, none did.

Solo sniffed more. This made no sense. Where were they?

With his head aching from being stuck in a confined space and the awkward angle he was forced to use, Solo decided to stretch. He stood up, forgetting that the box was leaning at a precarious angle above him. Solo is a strong, healthy dog, and even though the box was very heavy, it didn't take much for Solo to push it away from the wall as he stood up and send it crashing down with an almighty thud on the tiled, hallway floor.

Solo stood stock still, unsure what had happened. He looked around; no damage had taken place. The box had missed furniture and vases that Mum had dotted around. Which meant the box was now lying flat instead of leaning against the wall, spread out over Mum's favorite tile.

"This could have happened without me," Solo thought. Things fell by themselves all the time. Apart from the large hole now facing directly upwards and there for all to see, Solo was, in his mind, completely innocent.

Solo could have walked away at this moment and pretended that nothing that happened in the hallway was his doing, but he decided to look inside the hole now that he wasn't stuck at an awkward angle. Tilting his head sideways, using one eye and peering in as close as he could, all he could see was darkness, but he could still smell rubber and tennis balls.

This was far more temptation than a dog like Solo could stand. After all, what reasonable person could blame him for making a hole in the box in search of his favorite toy? No one, he decided.

Having justified his actions, Solo began tearing at the box in earnest. Big chunks of cardboard flew in all directions, but still no sign of any tennis balls. After a few minutes, with the hallway littered with discarded cardboard, he paused to look at his handiwork. The hole was now about half the size of the box, yet inside, all there appeared to be was rolled up sheets of some kind, wrapped in a thin layer of clear plastic.

Realizing that that there were probably no tennis balls in the first place, Solo sat back down on his haunches, disappointed and disgusted in the whole affair. All that hard work for nothing. He examined the contents of the box one more time, sniffing intently as he did so, and was about to walk away and take a well-deserved nap when he noticed something. Lying on top of the plastic sheet was a small length of red rope.

"This is interesting," thought Solo, for if he was able to pull on this rope, perhaps he could move whatever was in the box out the way. Then he would be able to double check to see if there were really no tennis balls underneath. He had come this far, he thought, so why not give it one more go.

Solo pulled on the short length of rope, but as strong as Solo was, he couldn't move the mysterious object it was attached to. He tried again, pulled, and pulled and pulled. Still no luck.

Slightly out of breath, Solo took a step back and surveyed the situation. He had no doubt now that he would be the one blamed for all the mess in the hallway, so he might as well at least get a shiny new tennis ball for his trouble. With a deep breath, he grabbed hold of the rope, and straining every muscle in his body, he pulled.

At first nothing happened, but then, ever so slowly the object began to move. Motivated by this event, Solo determined to keep going. Grunting with the effort, he gave an almighty tug.

Suddenly the rope was loose in his mouth, and for a split second he thought he had succeeded in moving the object out the way, but it hadn't moved. Instead, it seemed to grow before Solo's eyes. A loud hissing sound rose up from the depths of the box, followed by the now rapid expansion of the "thing" inside.

Solo backed away as best he could towards the front door, but no matter how much he backed away, the "thing" kept getting bigger and bigger, and the hissing noise kept getting louder and louder. Solo barked at it, just to remind it that Solo was in charge. The "thing" didn't listen.

Before he knew what was happening, Solo was backed against the front door by the giant rubbery thing. As it kept expanding, Solo could hear the sound of various vases and flowers falling over and crashing to the tiled floor. Suddenly Solo found himself lifted up and moved towards the front door by the ever expanding "thing" that still ignored Solo's barks to put him back down immediately.

As quickly as it had started, the hissing ceased, the "thing" stopped expanding, and there was quiet in the hallway. The only sound that could be heard was Solo's heavy breathing as he balanced on the giant rubbery edge of what he now understood to be an inflatable boat.

The front of the boat where Solo was balanced was wedged tightly against the front door, about four feet off the ground. The rest of the boat took up the entire hallway, back towards the kitchen. From where he was balanced, Solo could see some broken vases with their flowers scattered here and there, the hall side table had fallen over, and various keys and odds and ends had joined the flowers on the floor. The door to the front sitting room was entirely blocked by the boat, which had somehow managed to jam itself partially through the door.

Solo was just trying to figure how to get down from his perch when he heard a key in the lock behind him and the front door opened. "Opened" is the wrong word. With the weight of the boat and Solo pushing against the inside of the door, the door opened with an almighty *whoosh* as Solo and the front of the boat came tumbling out.

Dad, who had opened the door, was pushed back as the boat and Solo fell on him, knocking the cup of coffee Dad had in one hand to the ground. Then, the combined weight of Solo and the boat knocked the wind out of him. As soon as he landed on Dad's stomach, Solo rolled away with the boat continuing to rest on Dad's legs. Dad, who had not been thinking about anything in particular as he opened to the door, lay on his back staring in amazement at the front of his boat, pinning him to the ground, with Solo now standing, somewhat shakily, just beside him as Dad's coffee slowly drained into a nearby flower bed.

Quickly, Dad pulled his legs out from under the boat and stood up, not quite sure what was going on. Taking deep breaths as he tried to get some air in his lungs, Dad looked around. "What the...?" was all he could say as he rubbed is forehead in amazement, as if he thought he had gone completely mad. He stood there, unsure of his next move.

Solo, realizing the situation, rubbed up against Dad's leg, reminding Dad that he was there, and as if saying, "I'm as confused as you are."

Dad absentmindedly rubbed Solo's head. "Are you okay, boy? That must have been quite a shock. I'm sorry that happened." He continued to stroke Solo's head with one hand as he rubbed his own eyes with the other.

Solo nuzzled against Dad's knee in an attempt to communicate sympathy with the predicament Dad had got himself into. Both Solo and Dad knew that Mum would get upset at Dad for ordering such a dangerous piece of equipment, and Solo wanted Dad to know that he had his support through what was bound to be a trying few hours.

Through the years, the family would call this the "Amazing Boat Incident". In the telling of the story, Dad managed to get a huge boat inside the hallway of their house. Needless to say, Mum ensured that Dad got rid of the boat by making him give it to the local Boy Scout troop.

Solo felt quite guilty about this turn of events. Solo loved Dad and wouldn't do anything to get him in trouble, and he made a vow to never again give in to temptation. Until the next time.

11. Solo and the Missing Watch

Solo was hungry, so he was lying out in his usual spot under the large table in the family's kitchen. Solo had just been fed, but to Solo this was never enough, for if there was more food to be had, then he was always a willing recipient. And hanging around under the kitchen table while the family ate dinner, there was always a chance that someone would drop some food, ideally without noticing, allowing Solo to scoop up the proceeds without anyone being the wiser.

Today though, Solo was out of luck, as not one stray morsel of food dropped in his direction. Instead, he could hear the family discussing what to get one of the children's cousins for his birthday. He would be turning thirteen soon and various ideas were offered: clothing, a gift voucher for one of his favorite shops, some cash to spend how he chose, and so on.

These were all ideas that were thought of but discarded as unoriginal and uninspired. The family was about to move on to cleaning away the table when one of the children suggested getting their cousin a wristwatch. One with all sorts of alarm functions. Something modern, digital, and cool. The family all agreed this was an excellent suggestion, and Mum was charged with the task of picking one up next time she went into town.

Solo was a fan of birthdays. In particular his own, because even though he had been adopted and therefore his family didn't know his real birth date, they had made one up to closely represent his proper age. So on the 27th of September every year, Solo was given a new squeaky toy, a tube of tennis balls, and some new treats.

Even other people's birthdays excited Solo. Often he would wear a funny hat and a bright ribbon around his neck, which pleased him no end. Plus everyone seemed so happy, and even though Solo was not the one getting the presents, he was more than willing to join in the party games and try and get some forbidden birthday cake wherever possible. Yes, Solo liked birthdays.

A few days later after their breakfast meeting, Mum came home with the gift for her nephew, a very fancy digital watch. The children and Mum gathered around it, all slightly jealous. The watch was all black until the face was touched, at which point it would light up with all sorts of information.

They even showed it to Solo, who was fascinated by the sounds and lights it made, but as Solo couldn't read it was less interesting to him than it was to his family. What interested Solo most about the watch, however, wasn't the watch itself, but the strap, which appeared to be made of a type of hardened rubber. The watch was meant for hard outdoor use and was waterproof. The black rubber strap added a sense of toughness to the whole affair.

Solo, of course, always equated the smell of rubber with the existence of tennis balls. Or at least he used to, until not long ago when he discovered that rubber is used to make many things apart from simply tennis balls. Such as large boats, which he had inadvertently inflated in the family's hallway.

Besides, thought Solo, that was not his fault. The fact is the box the boat came in smelt like tennis balls, so it was hardly his fault he couldn't actually see anything from outside the box. What else was he supposed to do, apart from rip holes in the box to investigate?

In the case of the watch, Solo could clearly see that even though it smelled like a tennis ball, to his keen senses that is, he could see it was not a tennis ball. There was no chance Solo would make the same mistake twice. Mum left the watch in its box on her desk, and Solo thought nothing else about it, apart from catching the odd whiff of the rubber strap every now and then.

Soon the nephew's birthday arrived, and the present was wrapped, ready for him to swing by the house later that evening to be given his gift. Solo always liked having visitors, partially because he enjoyed their company, but mostly because they tended to make a great fuss over him, with lots of tummy rubs and praise about how handsome he was.

When Mum's nephew and parents showed up later that evening, everyone sang happy birthday with Solo joining in as best he could with the odd howl. After the new teenager had blown out the candles on his birthday cake, Solo's family gave him their present. The boy opened the box in anticipation. When he saw what was inside, he jumped up and down in excitement. Dad had set the watch to the right time, and placed it on the boys' wrist.

As the children gathered around to see the watch on their cousins' wrist, they were slightly envious. They both knew what they would be asking for Christmas.

Their cousin held his hand up so everyone could see how the watch looked. Even though Dad had tightened the strap as far as he could, the watch was still a loose fit on his nephew's wrist. Which meant it would fall down over the base of the boy's hand if he wasn't careful. His father told him they would get the strap adjusted at the local jewelers in the morning.

The rest of the evening was spent with the children playing board games, and Solo happily observing the activities from various vantage points around the house. Soon though, it was time for the children's cousin and his parents to leave. As they said goodbye at the door, Solo offered the cousin his paw to shake goodbye, a trick guaranteed to get a favorable reaction.

The boy shook Solo's paw, then looked down at the hand he was shaking with. The brand new watch was gone. Horrified, the boy leapt backwards and cried out in alarm.

Both families immediately started a panicked search for the missing watch. Some searched inside, and some outside in areas where the boy and his cousins had played earlier. Solo decided searching outside was far more fun than searching inside. So he was seconded into action, and tasked with using his keen sense of smell to help locate the watch.

At first Solo had no luck, but eventually he did manage to find two old, half-chewed tennis balls and an old sneaker, which he carefully carried back into the house with a sense of victory and his tail held high. His tail dropped when he was told that an old, moldy sneaker was not what they were all looking for.

Eventually it got dark and late enough that the kids had to go to bed. But not before Solo's family promised to look hard for the watch the next day and to call their cousin the moment they found the watch. A somewhat despondent family went to bed, leaving Solo alone to pace around the downstairs.

"On patrol," as Dad called it. "Perhaps Solo will get lucky and find the watch," he said to his wife as he turned out their bedroom light.

His wife sighed. Sometimes her husband's faith in Solo and his skills was quite annoying.

Downstairs, alone in the gloom, Solo wandered from room to room, attempting to find the watch by the smell of its rubbery band. Solo was upset that the cousin had lost the watch on the day of his birthday. He knew his family would do their level best to find the watch, but Solo was determined to be the one to hand it over. After all, he had all night.

But as much as Solo looked, smelled, sniffed, and prodded, he could not find the watch. Hearing the clock in the living room strike two, Solo knew it was time to call it a day; he would look again in the morning. But just as Solo was about to do his usual circular routine before laying down on his bed in kitchen, next to the nice and warm kitchen stove, he heard a noise.

At first, he wasn't sure what to make of it as it was quite faint. A plaintiff beeping seemed to be coming from somewhere. Any other noise in the house and it would probably be missed, but in the quiet of the dark, Solo, with his young ears, could hear it quite clearly.

He raised his head and sniffed the night. Nothing. Perhaps he should ignore it, he thought. After all, it was very late, he was tired, and he was sure there would be more adventures for him in the morning that would require his full attention. But as much as he tried, he could not ignore the beeping, which didn't seem to stop. Just a consistent *beep, beep, beep.*

Sighing to himself, Solo padded out of the kitchen in search of the noise. Whatever it was, it was keeping him from sleeping. And as sleep was always high on Solo's list of life's simple pleasures, he was determined to put a stop to that obnoxious sound as soon as possible.

He went into the living room, but the sound faded away. Next, he tried the dining room. The noise was louder, but still faint. Finally, he went into Mum's study where she did most of her writing. The noise instantly became louder.

Pausing for a moment to identify the location of the noise, he made his way over to Mum's office chair. Peering down as best he could into the chair, which was lit only by the light of the computer screen Mum had left on, Solo could now tell that the noise was coming from one of the folds within the seat of the leather chair.

To give himself room to investigate, he easily pushed the chair away from the desk, and then jumped up, placing his large, somewhat grubby front paws on the seat of the chair. Placing his nose closer to the chair and sniffing intently, he could now smell the rubber of the watchstrap.

"This has to be the watch," thought Solo as it continued its plaintiff plea to be found. Solo had no idea that watches could make such an annoying racket. Encouraged he dug down, and before long he emerged with the strap in his teeth with the watch itself dangling down.

Solo was extremely pleased with himself. He could see it now. In the morning, he would show the family the watch, and, boy, would they be pleased with him. Better yet, he could show them now! Take the watch to Mum and Dad's room, jump on the bed and show them. He had no doubt praise and tummy rubs would be thrown upon him by a grateful family. Perhaps they would even replenish his dwindling supply of tennis balls.

Just as Solo was thinking about his soon to be heroic reception, the chair which he had been resting his front legs on, rolled sharply away in its wheels, pushed by Solo's weight. Caught by surprise, Solo fell from the chair as it moved, causing his chin to come crashing down on the edge of the seat, which, even though it was heavily padded, caught him by surprise and made him bite down hard on his own tongue.

Solo jumped about the room in shock, and opened his mouth wide in surprised pain, but he forgot about the watch. Instead of falling to floor, it went directly into Solo's wide-open mouth. Before Solo could think, he swallowed the watch, the strap, everything. The beeping grew fainter and fainter as the watch moved down his throat and into his stomach, until it could no longer be heard.

Solo gulped. "Did what I think just happened, actually happen?" Solo thought to himself.

He tried to cough the watch back up, but nothing happened. What Solo did discover was that digital watches don't taste very pleasant. So he ran into the kitchen and drained his bowl of water. He then wiped his tongue on the kitchen floor in a futile attempt to get rid of the taste.

Now what was he supposed to do? He had found the watch, only to lose it, inside of himself no less. Highly embarrassed, Solo was grateful no member of his family was around to witness what had just happened.

Feeling as if he might have a stomachache coming on, Solo decided the best course of action was to go and have a well-deserved nap. Perhaps when he woke up in the morning, he would discover the whole situation was in fact a horrible dream.

Solo woke the next day to a roaring stomachache, which reminded him that what happened the night before was, unfortunately, not a dream. He wanted to tell his family what had happened, that he had in fact found the watch, but due to circumstances beyond his control and through no fault of his own, the watch was now safely ensconced inside Solo's own stomach.

Solo decided the best thing to do was not do anything that might implicate him in the watch's disappearance. Besides, even with all the will in the world, how could Solo even explain where the watch was? It was embarrassing enough to know the watch was inside of him, but he felt even worse when the family once again started to look for the watch, yet all the while it was only a few feet away.

The thought of the watch in his stomach had even put Solo off his usual hearty breakfast, which Mum noticed. "Solo didn't finish his food this morning," she told her husband at breakfast. "I hope I don't have to take him to the vet."

Dad grunted from behind his paper. "Solo has the constitution of an ox," he told his wife. "The only thing that will put Solo off his food is if he ate too much cake." He was referring to the time Solo had eaten some of Mum's best cake mix and promptly thrown it all up.

Solo, catching the sound of fatal word "vet", decided to make himself scarce and disappeared deep into the back garden for the rest of the morning while the family turned the house upside down in attempt to find the watch. In the end, Mum had to reach out to her nephew's parents and tell them they had no luck in locating it.

The rest of the morning was uneventful. This being a Saturday, the family went about their usual routine of sports fixtures for the kids. This would normally mean Solo would tag along in the back of the family SUV, but today, Solo didn't want to jump in, feeling quite sick to his stomach.

This caused Mum once again to remark that Solo could be sick. "If he isn't better by Sunday, I will take him to the vet. Doesn't he look pale to you?" she asked her husband.

"He's white," her husband replied. "He always looks pale."

The wife replied that her husband's remark was unhelpful, and that if he had nothing better to do, he should take their daughter to her soccer match.

At lunch that day, Solo remained under the table, listening to the family chat above him. Nothing of interest caught his attention, so he decided to try and take a nap. He had not slept much the night before, what with a watch and its rubber strap slowly making its way through his digestive system.

Solo had just fallen asleep when he was woken by a vibration in his stomach. At first, Solo thought it was severe indigestion caused by his unfortunate watch situation. But when the vibration in his stomach was followed by the incessant sound of beeping, Solo knew whatever was going on, it was much worse than simple indigestion.

All chatter in the table above him stopped. "Did you hear that?" one of the kids asked.

"Shush," said Dad. "Everyone, listen." And so they listened intently.

Then one by one, as the beeping continued, every member of the family stuck their head under the table and stared directly at Solo. Solo tried to pretend he was asleep, but it was no use.

"Oh, Solo!" cried out the entire family.

12. Solo Cracks the Case

Solo's village was all a flutter. It seemed that a series of burglaries at several homes and businesses were, according to the police, committed by the same person or gang. The entire village was on alert for suspicious strangers or activity. When a motorist had the misfortune to break down in the middle of the village, he was taken aback by the number of furtive glances he received from the local population, many of whom suspected him of "casing the joint".

Solo was in his usual spot under the large kitchen table, listening as his family discussed this spate of break-ins. When Dad told his family that a, "Cat burglar was on the prowl," Solo's first thought was, "Well that doesn't surprise me. Have you ever met a cat?" As far as Solo was concerned, cats were second only to squirrels in their chase-ability. Cats were to be regarded as highly capable enemies, more so than squirrels. For while squirrels were clever, fast and devious, cats were all those things and more. They had a serious extra advantage—claws!

Once Solo had chased a neighbor's cat under a parked car and, believing he had the cat cornered and in an attempt to show the superiority of dogs versus cats, stuck his snout under the car. The cat was ready and let Solo have it with a mighty whack from its claws, right on top of Solo's nose. The scratch was visible for over a week and, painful though his nose was, it was Solo's pride that was hurt most. Solo never underestimated cats after that.

While the idea of a "cat burglar" loose in the village was not a shock to Solo, and as much as wanted to help put the cat where he felt all cats belonged—in jail—he decided to leave the sleuthing to the police. The last thing Solo wanted was another sore nose.

Only a few days after hearing Dad use the phrase "cat burglar", Solo was highly disappointed to discover that this didn't mean an actual cat was the burglar. He learned the phrase referred to a clever burglar who would plan his crimes carefully and get away while leaving few clues behind. This didn't stop Solo from wondering why anyone would let cats off that easily.

Still, there was not much anyone could do in the village to capture the thieves, except to keep their eyes open for anything suspicious. Solo quite naturally decided the best he could do would be to continue to be Solo. Which meant taking naps, playing outside, chasing squirrels where possible, and avoiding contacts with cats.

Nothing much happened over the next week or so, and people in the village were beginning to think the spate of burglaries were over until Mr. Smith's, the grocer, was broken into.

"Why would anyone want to rob a grocer?" asked Mum upon hearing the news. "What are they going to do, steal a pound of carrots?"

Although it did turn out some money was taken, as far as Solo's family knew, nothing else was. The biggest expense was replacing a broken window. This new crime once again placed the whole village on edge, with the police no closer to catching the criminals.

It just so happened that the day after the break in, Mum needed to buy some vegetables. So she and Solo walked down to the village and into Mr. Smith's small shop. It turned out the criminals had taken more than just a small amount of money. An old necklace belonging to Mr. Smith's wife had been taken from its hook behind the counter.

"It's one of the few things that I have of hers, "said Mr. Smith. "Quite frankly, if they had taken more money and left that, I wouldn't feel as bad as I do now."

Mum nodded her head in sympathy. While Mum and Mr. Smith were chatting about the spate of criminal activity in the village, Solo was left to wander around.

Solo liked going into different stores, as each one had a unique smell. He particularly liked Mr. Smith's. As much as Solo would not eat anything green, he did like the scent that all the different types of vegetables gave off. And for a dog with Solo's keen sense of smell, it could sometimes be overpowering.

On this day though, as he wandered towards the rear of the shop, he noticed a different kind of smell, something that definitely wasn't usually sold in Mr. Smith's shop. Solo sniffed the air, attempting to pinpoint the source, and, picking up a stronger smell, he went to the back wall where the broken window had been boarded up. Solo sniffed the floor under the broken window. Solo couldn't quite put his paw on it. He knew he had smelled that smell somewhere before, but he just couldn't remember where. What he was certain of, though, was that it was a clue to the mystery of the break in at Mr. Smith's.

Solo had seen many detective shows, as he would often sit on the floor while the family watched television. He knew that the television detective always seemed to get their man and was often treated as a hero when they did. Solo made up his mind. He was going to solve the burglary of Mr. Smith's Green Grocers.

As he trotted beside Mum on his way home, Solo pondered on the smell he had picked up at the shop. He just knew he had smelled it somewhere. Still, right now, there were more important things on his mind.

It was time for dinner and perhaps a short nap before someone in the family took him for his evening walk. Or, if no one offered to take him, he would have to go into "extreme nagging mode", which meant pushing at people's elbows or legs until someone caved and said, "All riiight, Solo! Come on, let's go." Unfortunately, it was usually Dad who had to take Solo for a walk. The children would suddenly claim they had "mountains of homework", and Mum would mutter about having some bills to pay under her breath.

"Solo is *our* dog, you know," Dad yelled as he led Solo out the front door.

The next day, Solo had quite forgotten about solving the recent set of crimes in the village. He had a dream he had chased a squirrel and, realizing what fun it was, decided to go out into the back garden and look for a real squirrel to chase. Not finding one squirrel, Solo decided to take an extra nap or three, although he was quite annoyed that nothing was happening that would entertain him.

Nothing happened of any consequence in the village either, not until the following Saturday when the son had a football match for his school and the entire family, including Solo, went along to cheer on his team.

As usual, Solo was standing next to his family, watching the teams play, when he caught a slight whiff of the smell he had noticed before from the grocer's. At first Solo wasn't sure if he was imagining it, but there it was again. Using his keen, dog skill in identifying smells, Solo wandered away from the family and towards the smell.

Solo knew his family wouldn't notice him missing. After all, once he had gone for a walk all by himself for a whole day and the family was none the wiser. Solo wandered around the edge of the field behind the thin line of spectators until he came to a spot where the smell was the strongest. At first, he didn't notice anything and, once again, he thought he might be imagining it. He was about to give up, and head back to his family when he noticed someone familiar.

Standing not far away, with their backs to him watching the match, were the little boy and girl he had last seen in the middle of winter when they came by to play with the other children but had been too shy to simply go up and say hello. In order to encourage them to go and play, Solo had given the little boy a ride on his back as a way to introduce him and his sister to the other children. He had not seen them since that time. Standing next to the boy and girl was a woman who Solo assumed was their mother as she was holding the little boy's hand.

Slowly, Solo walked up behind the trio and sniffed again. No doubt about it, the smell he had picked up in the shop was the same one from the little boy and girl he had last seen a few months ago. And here he was now, picking up the same aroma. Solo let out his "pay attention to me" bark right behind the small family, making them jump. The little boy turned around and immediately recognized Solo.

"Look, Mama, look!" he yelled. "It's that nice dog again."

His mother and sister turned around. The girl, also remembering Solo, immediately placed her arms around his neck and gave him a big hug. Solo smiled in recognition, not worrying anymore about why their smell lingered at the grocer's. Whatever the reason the smell was there was no longer important to him.

The children's mother crouched down near Solo's head and gently stroked his velvet-like ear. "So you're the wonderful dog that gave my kids a great day." She looked at his name tag. "Solo. Where's your family, Solo? I presume they're here?"

Solo started walking back to his family the other side of the soccer field with the three—mother, daughter, and little boy —in tow. He came to a stop by his family, who had just realized he was no longer with them.

"Solo, where have you been?" said Mum. "How many times have I told you not to wander off like that" Oh, hello," she continued, realizing that Solo had bought guests. "I'm sorry, I didn't see you standing there." She shook hands with the children's mother and introduced them to her husband.

The little girl's and boy's mother explained what Solo had done a few months earlier and what a wonderful dog Solo is.

Dad muttered under his breath to his wife, "Yeah, but she doesn't have to live with Solo, now, does she?" His wife gently elbowed him in the ribs and smiled at the family.

On the way home, Solo was able to learn much more about the new family. It turned out they had just arrived in the village and were living in what Dad described as a "shack" on the edge of the village. In reality, it was a very small, run down cottage, but Solo got the general idea. The family didn't have much money, and the mother was looking for work. However, the little boy had insisted on asking if Solo could come over to his house sometime soon, and Mum, having invited the boy and girl to play at her house, said that next time she was walking Solo, she would drop by.

The opportunity for Mum and Solo to pay a visit to the small family didn't occur for about a week or so, but as promised, when Mum was taking Solo for his "long walk", she and Solo walked up to the front door. The mother let them in, and Solo was let off his lead. The children took Solo into the small, slightly scruffy back garden to play fetch while Mum and the mother chatted over a cup of tea.

Solo had a great time playing with the children, partially because he liked them immeasurably, and partially because they seemed to have a good supply of old tennis balls. After about half an hour of play, the children realized Solo was thirsty and bought him in to give him a drink of water. As he bent down to drink out of an old cracked bowl, Solo noticed something that had fallen under the small kitchen table. It was a small necklace which Solo recognized immediately. It was the necklace Mr. Smith used to keep behind his cash register as a reminder of his wife.

Solo's first instinct was to pick it up and take it to Mum, but something told him not to. He simply stood there, head near the bowl, pretending he was still going to drink some more water.

Just then, Mum yelled, "Come on, Solo, time to go," as she stood by the open front door.

"Don't worry, I'll get him," he heard the children's mother say, and she walked into the kitchen.

Solo looked up at her and dropped the necklace at her feet. The mother turned bright red and quickly picked it up and stuck it in her pocket. Solo stood and stared at her with one of his unblinking looks, which he was uncommonly good at.

After what seemed like forever, the mother whispered,
"Thank you Solo."

That evening, Solo listened as Mum told Dad about the
visit and what a nice family they had spent time with. It seemed
they had fallen on hard times and had moved into the rundown
cottage because it was cheap and the mother wanted to give the
children a fresh start.

Dad was surprised to learn that Solo had been well behaved. "Wonders will never cease," he told his wife.

A few weeks later, Solo was back with Mum at Mr. Smith's grocers, when Mum noticed the old silver necklace back behind the counter, hanging in its usual spot. "Well," said Mum, "wherever did you find that?"

"It was taped to the front door in a brown envelope," said Mr. Smith, "along with a note apologizing for the break-in. They even returned the money. I suppose they felt bad, although I didn't care about the money, just the necklace."

That night, as Solo lay in his usual spot under the large kitchen table, he thought about the little family on the edge of the village and how desperate the mother must have been to take the risks she did. Whatever the reason, Solo decided it was best not to judge people, as until you have all the details, you can never be sure why people do the things they do. Solo also decided that being a dog made life quite simple. All he needed was a loving home, a place to play, and the odd squirrel to chase every once in a while.

"What could life do to improve on that?" he thought as he did his usual circular motion before he lay down to get a good night's rest.

13. Solo the Matchmaker

Solo was watching the world go by through the open front door. He was lying down on the cool tile in the hall just inside the front door, which his family had left open in a desperate attempt to let some air into the stuffy house. Today was forecast to be the hottest day of the year so far, and even though it was early, the temperature was already climbing. In order to get ready for the heat, Solo had bagged the coolest spot in the house before any other member of his family did. Not that they were likely to want to sit on the hard tile, but Solo wasn't taking any chances. You just never knew what humans might do.

Solo lay there, peering out down the drive to the quiet street and into the open field beyond. The field where he had famously driven the family car with the local vicar clinging to the front. Solo thought about that day, and while he didn't want to repeat driving a car across a muddy field with a screaming vicar attached, at least that day hadn't been so hot.

He continued to stare outside, wondering if anything was ever going to happen, when he heard a familiar sound. It was the unmistakable sound of a bicycle being peddled down the lane in front of Solo's house. More importantly, Solo recognized this particular bike. It was the young vicar's.

It hadn't escape Solo's notice that every time the vicar rode past his house, he did so at a high rate of speed. If you paid special attention, you could hear the bike slow down as it approached Solo's home, then as it drew close to the driveway, it would suddenly speed up. If you were looking just at the right time, all that seemed to pass was a blur of a vicar, bent over the handlebars in attempt to gain a better pace, his legs frantically peddling as fast as they could.

Solo knew why this was. In addition to driving the vicar on the front of a car and depositing him into a muddy pond, Solo had on several other occasions caused the vicar pain and anguish. Not that Solo meant to cause pain and anguish; it just seemed to happen that way. And even though Solo knew why the vicar would want to avoid any other run ins with him, it still hurt Solo's feelings slightly to know that a human, any human, would not want to spend time with him.

Solo watched out the window and, soon enough, the vicar appeared going as fast as he could, not looking ahead, but making sure Solo wasn't around to take him by surprise. As has been said, Solo understood the vicar's anxious glances towards his house, but also felt that if only the vicar got to know Solo a little better, he too would come to love Solo. Just like his family.

Of course, if you asked the vicar if he could ever want to know Solo better, the resounding answer would be, "No." Still, this didn't prevent Solo from wondering what he could do to get the vicar to change his mind about him. And once Solo makes up his mind about something, well, just about anything can happen.

A few weeks went by and Solo had not seen the vicar once. Not even on one of his regular walks into town with a member of his family. That is until, one day, a few weeks later, Solo saw the vicar in the village, talking to a very pretty girl. Or rather, the vicar was attempting to talk to a very pretty girl.

Clearly the vicar was extremely nervous. His face was red and perspiring. He kept rubbing his hands together one minute, then stuffing them in his pockets the next. It was as if he couldn't make up his mind what to do with them.

Solo could tell the conversation wasn't going well. The girl kept looking at her watch and glancing around as if she was looking for an escape route. Or someone to come and rescue her.

After what seemed like an eternity, the girl made her excuses and left. The vicar took out a large white handkerchief and mopped his sweaty brow, looking around sheepishly as if to make sure no one had noticed his abject failure with a member of the opposite sex.

Solo observed all this from across the street. He felt sorry for the vicar, who obviously liked the girl. Yet he seemed too nervous to even be able to carry out a normal conversation. Solo thought of his friendship with Sunny, the poodle that lived next to his house. Solo thought how wonderful it was to have a friend you could count on. A friend who was a girl. Even if she was a fussy poodle whose full name was Sunshine Rays Beauty Lady Smyth-Johnson .

Solo made up his mind that, somehow, he was going to bring the vicar and the girl together. After all, he and Sunny had been friends for some time now. How hard could it be for Solo to help the vicar? It never once occurred to Solo that the vicar would have been horrified at the thought of Solo's unsolicited help.

That night, as the family watched television, Solo sat in his usual spot under the kitchen table, trying to think of a way to help the vicar, but no ideas came. Deciding he needed a change of atmosphere, Solo wandered into the living room and lay down on the floor in front of the TV. He had closed his eyes in order to take a short, refreshing nap before bedtime when his ears pricked up. Something interesting was being said on the television.

Mum and Dad were watching a program about cooking. Both of them enjoyed these shows immensely. Mum because she enjoyed cooking some of the new recipes shown on television. And Dad because he enjoyed eating, mostly, what Mum cooked.

One of the presenters on the show was talking about how she and her husband first became friends when they realized they both enjoyed cooking. Solo's mind began to race. Of course! If he was going to help the vicar with the young lady, he had to find out what they had in common. If they knew that about each other, perhaps then they would become friends and the vicar wouldn't be as nervous when he talked to her.

There was, quite naturally, a huge flaw in Solo's worthwhile plan. He had no idea what the pretty girl liked to do, and even though he thought he knew the vicar quite well, he had no idea what the vicar enjoyed either. All Solo knew about the vicar was that he rode his bike a lot, that he grew vegetables, and that he held church services once a week in front of about fourteen people and a few pigeons.

The pigeons found their way inside the church from the belfry and would sit, just out of the reach of the vicar and his broom, as he attempted to shoo them away. They would *coo* quite loudly, often just as the vicar was getting warmed up about the sins of gluttony or something similar.

Solo lay in front of the television, not paying any attention to what was happening on the screen. His mind was elsewhere. He knew now how to get the vicar and the girl together. He knew the vicar rode his bike all the time. He didn't have a car. Perhaps the girl had a bike too? The problem was Solo didn't know anything about riding a bike. It looked extremely uncomfortable. Perhaps the girl attended the church services. Had they met that way?

Solo made up his mind that, come Sunday morning, he would put in an appearance at the church to see if the girl was there. If she was, well, Solo had absolutely no idea what he would do, but he was pretty sure whatever he decided to do, he would think of something amazing to bring the vicar and pretty girl together.

Sunday morning came and his family was still asleep. As was usual when the family had a lazy day, Solo would jump up on Mum and Dad's bed, which is something he wasn't normally allowed to do. But when the kids didn't have school and Mum and Dad didn't have work, Solo found they were too keen on sleeping in to shoo him off. Except today, Solo wasn't interested in just lying there. He needed a member of the family to let him out so he could go to the church, which was conveniently located just down the road.

Solo jumped on Mum and Dad's bed. And as usual, they ignored him. Dad mumbled something about, "GettoffmyfeetSolo," but that was about it.

This wouldn't do. Solo was in a hurry to see if the pretty girl attended the vicar's Sunday service. He moved around on the bed, doing one of his famous circular movements, hoping to get their attention. All he heard was a soft snore from Mum and a louder snore from Dad. Solo took action. He walked over to the top of the bed, making sure to walk on Dad as much as possible, then lay down, putting his full weight on Dad's head.

Dad woke up with a start. All he knew was a giant, hot, furry pillow type thing was pressing down on his head. "What the...?" he gasped, searching for air. "Solo!" Dad sat up, forcing Solo to slide onto his wife's head.

"What on earth's going on?" said Mum as she too sat up, forcing Solo to lay between them.

He simply stared at them both, using what he thought was his best smile.

"What's he smiling at?" asked Dad. "He's never sat on my head before."

"Perhaps he needs to go out?" said Mum. She gently stroked Solo's head before laying back down and saying. "Let him out, dear."

Dad looked at his wife, who was already fast asleep, and then at Solo. "All I want is one day a week when I don't need to get up," he said to himself.

"Unless it's golf," he heard Mum say, who was clearly pretending to be asleep.

"Very funny," said Dad as he staggered out of bed, rubbing the sleep from his eyes. "Come on, you," he said to Solo. "I suppose when you have to go, you have to go."

Gingerly, with both eyes only half open, Dad walked downstairs to the kitchen with Solo padding softly behind. Dad unbolted the kitchen door and, leaving it half open, Solo wandered outside. Dad watched as Solo went onto the back lawn, presumably to do whatever it was Solo liked to do.

Dad sighed. He had been in the middle of an amazing dream where he won his golf club's over-forty tournament and was about to be presented with the overly large trophy when Solo woke him up. As Dad went back upstairs, hoping to be able to fall back to sleep, he wondered, not for the first time, why did he ever agree to get a dog? Particularly Solo!

Free at last to pursue his plan, Solo quickly went to the front of the house and down the road to the small church. He peered around the hedge and up the path which led to centuries-old church door. As he looked, he could see a small crowd of parishioners chatting outside, waiting for their turn to enter the church. Solo decided it would be best to wait until everyone had gone inside. He had learned from experience that humans, in particular grown-up humans, were sometimes picky about where dogs would be allowed to go.

Solo waited patiently until the last of the parishioners had gone in. Seeing the coast was clear, he walked down the small path, past the old graveyard, and was about to peer into the church when he heard a noise. Turning his head, he was just in time to see the pretty girl ride her bike down the path, throw it down on the grass, and run into the church. She was in such a hurry, she ignored Solo completely.

Solo paused for a moment, then gently pushed open the old door with his nose. The small church was built hundreds of years ago. It had an old, stone floor and about a dozen rows of old, wooden pews with an aisle down the middle. This was not Solo's first visit to the church however.

Not that long ago, he had chased a squirrel into the church; the resulting chaos had made front page news in the local newspaper and caused major embarrassment for the vicar. Although Solo had helped raise money for the church. Still, this was one reason Solo was determined to make things right with him.

Solo stood at the back of the church, which was lit by a few lights, a couple of candles, and some beautiful stained-glass windows. Solo could see the small congregation near the front. No one had noticed Solo. But Solo had found the girl.

She was not sitting near the front like the rest; she was sitting on the last row, as if she wanted to appear not too keen to be there. Clearly, she was shy. Solo walked down the aisle, just so he could get a better look at the vicar and hear better what he was saying.

As he walked by the girl's row, she turned and saw this big, almost pure white dog, slowly walking down the aisle, seemingly without a care in the world. The girl's mouth fell open as she stopped listening to the vicar's sermon, which she just knew would be the best ever in the history of sermons, and watched as Solo continued to walk slowly down towards the vicar.

Solo didn't have a plan. He rarely did. All he knew was that the vicar and the girl belonged together, and here they were in the same church. All he had to do was to make *them* realize they belonged together. How hard could that be for dog like Solo?

Perhaps if he made himself known to the vicar, the vicar would laugh and explain to the congregation how it was Solo who had help raise enough money to rebuild part of the church. Then with the mood lightened, the girl might feel more comfortable coming down to the front of the church. The vicar and girl's eyes would meet, and that would be that. At least, that was Solo's idea. And as it was his only idea at that point, he simply decided to run with it.

He continued to walk slowly down the aisle, the girl's eyes following him as he went. As he neared the front of the church, the vicar, speaking from the lectern, was just about to make his rousing speech on the subject of greed. He had noticed the pretty girl enter the church, as she had done the past few Sundays, and he was determined to deliver his finest sermon ever.

He opened his mouth to deliver his most passionate words that morning when suddenly he noticed Solo nearing the first row of pews. The small congregation, apart from the girl, had not noticed Solo. They were too enraptured in the vicar's sermon, who seemed to be on fire this morning.

More than one parishioner wondered if the vicar had drunk too much coffee, as excitable as he seemed. Regardless of why the vicar was all fired up that morning, they were all looking forward to his conclusions on the subject of greed. Some even leaned forward, as if to try and make themselves just that little bit closer to the words of wisdom that were, no doubt, soon to leap from the vicar's mouth.

The vicar took his breath. The congregation waited. And, just as the vicar was about to deliver the dynamic conclusion, there was Solo. Grinning from ear to ear, looking directly at the vicar, using the unblinking stare which was all too well known to members of his family. The vicar could not take his eyes from Solo's; he felt they were having a hypnotic effect.

The vicar fumbled for his notes, his momentum lost. The congregation waited patiently. Perhaps the vicar took this pause to build up the tension before his final onslaught.

The vicar paused, attempted to compose himself, and tried again. He glanced up, attempting to look at the back of the church. Attempting to speak directly to the girl. But he couldn't help it. He was drawn once again to the smiling, unblinking face of Solo.

Suddenly the vicar's mind was filled with images of Solo chasing a squirrel through his church, yet somehow ending up on the front page of the newspaper. Again. Or the time the vicar was clinging to the front of a car with Solo in the driver's seat. It was all too much.

Now, totally flustered, all that came out of the vicar's mouth was, "Um," as he looked around desperately for inspiration while he fumbled with his notes.

Solo, not understanding why the vicar had stopped talking, decided to take a closer look. He walked towards the pulpit, then sat back on his haunches, looking directly up at the vicar. Solo's intention was to make sure the vicar noticed the girl at the back of the church, but unfortunately, Solo was having the opposite effect.

By now the entire congregation had noticed Solo and were whispering among themselves. The vicar had lost his audience completely.

Just then, the girl at the back of the church decided to take matters into hand. She slowly walked down the aisle, went up to Solo, and led him to the back of the church, but not before giving the vicar the most amazing smile he'd ever seen.

The vicar tuned bright red. But now, knowing the girl of
his dreams was on his side, he found new confidence. Picking up
his scattered notes, he gave the rousing conclusion to his
sermon that he had been attempting all along.

At the back of the church, the girl looked at Solo's name on his collar. "Thank you Solo," she whispered in his ear, as he lay at her feet on the stone floor. "I don't think I would have had the courage." She scratched his head.

Solo smiled. He was not sure what he had done, but whatever it was, it seemed to have worked out.

After the service, the girl and the vicar walked Solo home. His family was barely awake when they dropped Solo off with Mum.

Dad drank deeply into his cup of black coffee as Mum told the story. "Why am I not surprised?" he asked no one in particular. "Solo goes to church, interrupts a service, and then makes two strangers bring him home. And we will never know why." He sighed. Perhaps he should go back to bed. The day was still young, and there was still plenty of time left for Solo to cause mayhem and pandemonium.

Solo, though, was having a totally different thought. Earlier, as the girl and the vicar had walked back down the drive, he had noticed them, very gently and very shyly, holding hands. Maybe they were strangers once, he thought, but not anymore.

14. Solo and the Surfer

Solo's family had rented a small cottage close to the beach for a quick break before the children had to go back to school after the long summer. Solo always liked the beach. He liked running through the surf, rolling in the damp sand, even swimming a little. What he really liked however was being part of the family's activities, playing fetch or trying to catch a Frisbee.

His family enjoyed having Solo with them too, it was fun to watch him become more and more excited the closer they got to the beach. His bark would get louder and louder. And, just sometimes, on the drive there, Solo would be allowed to sit on one of the passenger seats and stick his head out of the window. The wind distorting his beautiful face, and sometimes, a fly would be pushed right up his nose, causing him to sneeze loudly.

Once, when this had happened, Solo sneezed so violently that large amounts of phlegm shot out of his nose, along with the now dead fly, and directly into the daughter's hair. The daughter proceeded to scream so loudly at this catastrophic event that the noise from the open window was drowned out by her yelling.

Passengers in nearby cars turned to see what all the fuss was about. Another dog, who also had his head out of the window, gave Solo a puzzled look as they drove by. Such was the commotion that Dad was forced to pull over while Mum did her level best to get oodles of sticky Solo goo-mucus and the dead fly remains out her daughter's hair.

After a half hour, the family were on their way again, but not before Dad was forced to buy some big ice cream cones loaded with many flavors of ice cream just to calm the family's nerves. Solo was once again banished to the rear cargo area of the SUV after the children refused to have him sit with them. This didn't stop Solo from leaning over the back seats and grabbing the remains of the ice-cream cone from the daughter, who promptly yelled that Solo had stolen her ice cream while she in turn tried to grab her brother's ice cream.

Mum and Dad, who were by now thoroughly fed up with the whole trip, told the kids to stop complaining as they would be at the cottage soon. But, as they got closer, the road changed into twisty, narrow, country lanes. The rolling motion of the car in the twists and turns had an unfortunately side effect on Solo, whose stomach was not handling eating ice cream too well. Within a few minutes the ice cream was no longer in his stomach, but all over the back of the children's heads as he threw up not only the ice cream, but the remains of his rather large breakfast.

Once again, Dad was forced to stop as he and Mum cleaned up the mess. The children's heads were rinsed with some bottled water, and after a few minutes, they were on their way again. But not before Dad said to his wife, and not for the first time, "Whose idea was it we get a dog?" Forgetting as he did in these circumstances, that *he* was the one that had chosen Solo.

Eventually, they made it to the seaside cottage, where the daughter immediately insisted her mother wash her hair to get the final remnants of Solo's vomit and mucus out.

Even though evening was closing in, the family was able to make it down to the beach before it got dark. The family set up camp on some towels so the kids could swim and splash around, and Dad could take what he felt was a thoroughly deserved nap before bedtime. Something Solo was quite good at. Solo splashed and swam with the children. If they thew a ball, he would chase it down, even if it went into the ocean. When they played Frisbee, Solo did his darnedest to catch it mid-flight.

It was during one of his attempts to grab the Frisbee, that he noticed the most amazing thing. Grown men and women riding the waves on what, to him, looked like large pieces of brightly colored wood. They were standing up and leaning in different directions to steer.

Solo thought this looked like a lot of fun. Not only that, it looked incredibly easy. How hard could it be, to stand on a piece of wood and ride it to shore? Solo decided he needed to try this too.

The snag was that no member of Solo's own family had been thoughtful enough to bring along one of these pieces of wood. So Solo simply stopped and stared as these people paddled their way out into the ocean, picked a wave, then they would paddle quickly and, as the wave picked up speed, they would stand up and ride it all the way to the beach. This looked totally awesome! Solo just *knew* he could do this too.

That night, as he slept in the small kitchen at the cottage, Solo had a dream he was riding what he soon learned was called a surfboard. In his dream, he rode it all the way to the shoreline, with an admiring family watching his every move.

The next morning as Solo stretched himself awake, he made up his mind that he was going to see if someone would let him have a go at surfing. Solo also knew he a major advantage over humans. They were able to balance with just two legs; Solo had four legs. Surely that would make the whole exercise much easier to learn. Really, how hard could it be?

As the family made their way back to the beach, Solo started thinking about this surfing thing. While he had absolutely no doubt he could not only surf, but surf well—Solo rarely doubted his own skills—he knew he had to overcome two problems. Firstly, he needed access to a surfboard. Secondly, he needed a human to push him out on the board so he could ride it back in.

While he thought he might be able to push the board out by gripping it in his teeth, he knew even for a strong, young dog like Solo, that this might be too much to ask. Therefore, he would have to rely on the kindness of humans to push him out.

Solo knew how to make humans like him and get them to do things for him. He knew they tended to find him endearing, what with his big black eyes, almost pure white fur, and his general relaxed demeanor. If he pulled all his tricks, such as laying on his back looking for tummy rubs and putting out one his giant paws to shake, someone was bound to see if he wanted to ride a surfboard. Well, that was plan anyway.

As the family set up camp, Solo scanned the beach looking for a likely candidate of his charm campaign. Even though it was early, quite a few surfers were in the water, taking advantage of some the larger waves bought on by some gusting winds. Most of the surfers were too busy to notice Solo as he paraded up and down the beach just by the shoreline. He was hoping that one of them would notice him, and if they did so, he would put out a paw for them to shake. If he did this, he theorized, they would be won over, and before too long, he would be riding the waves like a pro.

Alas, not one surfer, either in the ocean or walking along the beach with their boards under one arm, paid the slightest bit of attention to Solo. What Solo couldn't have possibly known, as he couldn't read, was that later that day, there was to be a surfing competition. A small podium had been erected further up the beach for the judges of the surfing competition. A large sign attached to the podium read, "Today, Ultimate Surfing Competition." No matter how charming he tried to be, they were too focused on getting ready for the competition.

Solo decided to give up on getting to try a surf board, at least for a while. He was a very determined dog, and he was not going to let this setback get in the way of his objective. Still, he knew when to take a break, so he wandered back to his family, lay down beside Dad, and decided to take a nap. He hadn't closed his eyes for long when he heard the children calling him from the edge of the beach.

"Come and play Frisbee, Solo," they shouted.

Solo didn't need asking twice. If he couldn't surf, he could certainly play Frisbee with the kids. Solo ran over to the children, who were playing in the low water, and noticed a surfboard floating on the edge of the surf being slowly pushed up the beach by the water. Solo didn't need an invitation.

Immediately he ran over to the board and gingerly placed one paw on it. So far so good. Then another. Finally, he was standing completely on the board. It bobbed gently, the base of the board now scraping on the sand thanks to Solo's weight.

Solo may not have been out in the ocean, "riding the waves" as the children had put it, but this was the next best thing. Even though he wasn't actually moving—he was, after all, simply rocking from side to side as the waves came in—he was in heaven. He could now say he had ridden a surfboard, which is more than many dogs could say.

He couldn't wait to get home and explain to his friend and neighbor, Sunny the Poodle, what he had done. Would she have done this? Solo thought for a second. Knowing Sunny's adventurous spirit, he knew the answer was yes. Still, he had done it first.

Just then, the owner of the surfboard came back to pick it up, and seeing Solo on the board, stopped still in amazement. "Well now, that's interesting," he muttered. "Whose dog is this?" he said loudly to no one in particular.

The children, who were still close by, came up to the young man who asked the question. "He's Solo, and he's our dog," they said.

"Well, he's on my board, and he won't get off," said the young man.

He was correct. During all this, Solo had not moved. He was afraid that if he got off, he might never have the chance to get back on a board again.

Solo remained still. Solo remained balanced. Solo remained ready to surf.

The children told Solo to, "Get off now!"

Solo didn't move. They pulled his collar. Solo didn't move. They tried to push him off the board. Solo didn't move. Finally, the kids went and got Dad, who was none too pleased about having been woken up from his nap.

"Come on, Solo. Now!"

Solo knew he was licked. Besides, he couldn't stay on the board forever. Begrudgingly he got off, head low. His chance at surfing glory was gone for good.

The young man gladly picked up his surfboard, but as he turned to go back into the ocean to continue practicing for the competition, he noticed the disappointed look on Solo's face. So he turned to Dad and said, "Clearly your dog likes the idea of surfing. I'll tell you what I'll do. Once the competition is over later, I'll let him have a go. Okay?"

Dad thanked him profusely, and Solo put out a paw for the man to shake. Solo was a very polite dog.

That afternoon, the family watched the surfing competition from their vantage point on the beach. It was all very exciting, with the waves getting larger and more ferocious as the afternoon progressed. The family was rooting for the young man, who amazingly, was in a close race for first place. It all came down to one more go for him and another man. The family watched as both men gave their final shots at winning the competition.

Solo, deciding he couldn't sit still any longer, ran down to the edge of the beach, and started barking his encouragement to the young man. The crowd on the beach delighted in Solo's contribution, and just like a coach encouraging his team to win, the more Solo barked his encouragement, the louder the crowd became. Solo's bark would go up an octave, and then down an octave in excitement. Up and then down. Up and then down. The crowd loved it. Although anyone trying to take a nap on the beach would surely have been woken up.

Finally, the young man finished his run, and came ashore, tousling Solo's head as he ran by him. Everyone waited with bated breath as the judges on their raised platform discussed the final results.

The young man was announced the winner, by just a single point. But it was enough. And a win is still a win. He shook hands with the runner up, who was clearly very disappointed.

Solo's family were very pleased for the winner. Solo, who didn't understand the rules of the competition whatsoever, was simply delighted that his family seemed pleased for the young man. But he was also delighted at the thought of having a go at surfing. But the young man, surrounded by well-wishers, left beach without saying a word to Solo.

Solo watched him leave and bowed his head.

"Never mind, Solo," said Dad as he watched the young man walk away with his surf board under his arm. "He probably forgot, what with all the excitement of winning. I'm sure we'll see him again before long."

Solo hoped Dad was right. He had really looked forward to surfing.

Soon the family packed up and went back to their little cottage. As Solo lay on his bed in the kitchen, he thought about the day and how promising it had all been, only to end in disappointment.

Over the next few days, the family went down the beach often, and they watched as various surfers showed off their skills. The young man wasn't one of them. Solo played Frisbee and splashed in the surf, but he couldn't get out of his mind that he had missed an opportunity to do something that he would probably never have the chance to do again.

Soon it was the last afternoon on the last day for the family at the beach. The children and Mum and Dad played in the ocean. Solo didn't really feel like joining in; he was going to take a nap. He knew he would eventually get over not learning to surf, as Solo was a very happy dog, but that still didn't take away his disappointment at that moment.

Solo closed his eyes and dreamt he was winning the All Dog Surfing Competition. In his dream, he was just about to be awarded a trophy that was bigger than he was when he was awakened by a familiar voice.

"Solo, Solo. Wake up, boy," said Dad. "There's someone here to see you."

Solo opened one eye. It was the young man, still carrying his surfboard under his arm. The young man knelt down and put out his hand. Solo put out his paw.

"Solo," said the young man, "this is my girlfriend, Samantha."

For the first time, Solo noticed a young woman standing behind the man. "She tells me you were the one encouraging the crowd to get loud. I wanted you to know that I heard the noise, and it encouraged me to do my best. You helped me win Solo!"

Solo beamed with pride.

"So, Solo," the young man continued, "I promised you a go on the surfboard, and that is precisely what we're going to do. Come on!"

Solo, the young man, his girlfriend, and Solo's entire family went down to the sea. There, Solo jumped on the surfboard while the young man paddled him out into the ocean. After about a minute, he followed Solo in, carefully holding the board for him, as a wave took Solo back to the beach. They did this a few times more, and then, before Solo even knew it, the young man let go of the board, and Solo rode into the beach all by himself.

Solo was beside himself with excitement. This was literately the best thing he had ever done. Well, that and eat ice cream. Or ride in a motorcycle sidecar. Or drive a car...or... Solo simply decided to add surfing to the list of *one* of the best things he had ever done. Later, as the young man said goodbye and walked away holding hands with Samantha, Solo, not for the first time, felt it was good to be Solo.

A few days later, with the family back home, an exhausted Mum and Dad were finally able to sit down and watch some of the video they had taken from their trip. "I thought trips to the beach were supposed to be relaxing," said Dad. "But taking kids and Solo, well, that's not relaxing at all."

He pressed play on his phone as he and Mum watched some clips from their trip. The last video was of Solo riding the surfboard with no help from the young man.

"Well," Said Mum, "you have to admit, Solo certainly made the most of the trip."

"Typical," said Dad. "Trust Solo to become the hero to someone. But at least he wasn't on the front page of the newspaper...again."

Dad was wrong. Solo was on the front page of a
newspaper. A national surfing magazine had covered the
competition and had a photograph of the young man arriving at
the shore after his winning run. And who was there, in the
photo? Why, Solo of course.

15. Solo and the School Concert

It was a busy time in Solo's household. Both the children were busy getting ready for the school concert. The show was put on twice a year by the kids' school and was designed to show off each child's talent. In the case of the children in Solo's household, the brother was to play the guitar, and his sister the flute.

The boy enjoyed playing the guitar, even if it was an acoustic version and not electric. He really wanted an electric one, so he could make more noise, but so far his parents had resisted. At some point they knew they would have to get him one, but only when Dad had finished the workshop at the end of their property.

At least there, "We won't have to hear him," said Dad.

His sister on the other hand did not want to learn the flute at all. In fact, she wanted absolutely nothing to do with any musical instrument whatsoever. "I watch music on my phone," she'd say. "Why do I have to play anything?"

Her parents had suggested the violin instead. She had said, "No!" in absolute disgust. The guitar, they suggested. Again, no. Her brother was already playing that. She certainty didn't want to play anything her *brother* was playing. The trumpet? Again, no.

After several weeks of arguing, her parents had eventually insisted on the flute, primarily as Mum could help given that she also learned when she was at school. And secondly, because her parents felt it wouldn't be as damaging to their sanity to hear her learn the flute as it might be the violin or the trumpet. As it transpired, the school offered lessons, so the family did not have to endure the children learning their instruments as much as they had anticipated.

Solo had only ever caught the sound of the guitar. He had yet to hear girl playing the flute. This was not because he had just been out of earshot. It was because the daughter had refused to practice at home, lest her annoying older brother make fun of her.

But, with the date of the school concert getting closer, both children had to increase the amount of practice. This meant some practice at home. The first time Solo caught the sound of the flute was when he was the bottom of the garden, right where Dad was attempting to grow some vegetables.

Dad had pulled out some carrots, which didn't resemble carrots at all. They were as thin and stringy as a piece of wire. The only thing that made them seem like they might, in a different life, be carrots, is that they were orange. Dad showed one to Solo, who sniffed it gingerly. "See, Solo, you'd think I'd be able to grow some carrots. But look at them. What am I doing wrong?"

Solo had no idea what Dad was doing wrong, but when Dad tossed the sorry looking carrot to the ground so Solo could eat it, he took one bite and spat it out. While Solo had no idea what Dad's failure was in the carrot growing department, he was sure of one thing. Even if Dad had succeeded in growing carrots successfully, why on earth would anyone want to eat them?

Dad looked at the remains of the carrot Solo had spat out. "That bad, huh, boy?" He picked the rest of the carrots; they were all as equally pathetic. "Time to start over, Solo. Perhaps I didn't water them enough?"

Again, Solo wasn't interested in something so disgusting. Instead, he was about to nudge Dad on the knee to encourage him to take him for a walk rather than waste all this time growing carrots when a strange sound drifted across the lawn and down to Dad's vegetable garden. Solo had never heard it before. It was a high-pitched sound that seemed to go directly through his brain. And even though much of it was out of tune, Solo found it quite exhilarating.

Dad, on the other hand, had a different perspective. "Probably a good idea we're as far away from that noise as possible. Right, Solo?"

Solo wasn't really listening to Dad; he was instead listening intently to the enchanting music emanating from the house. He decided he wanted to join in and was just about to "sing" along when the sound stopped and was replaced by yelling. Even from this distance, Dad and Solo could tell it was the children arguing.

It soon became obvious that the boy had made fun of his sister's flute skills. At which point she'd thrown the flute down with a thud on the floor, stormed upstairs, making sure to stamp every step as she went, and then slammed her bedroom door. All the while yelling at her mother that she'd wished she never ever, ever had a brother. Or, barring that, wishing that she herself had never been born.

Dad decided to return to the house, thinking, quite correctly as it turned out, that his wife might need reinforcements. Solo trotted happily beside him. He was anxious to get to his water bowl. He needed to get the aftertaste of that horrible carrot out of his mouth.

When they arrived at the back door, Mum was drinking a nice strong cup of tea. "To calm my nerves," she said. "Whose ideas was it to have children?" she asked her husband.

Dad thought it best not to say it was her idea. He would have been quite happy with a dog.

As the day of the school concert drew closer, the children decided to do most of their practicing at school. That way they could avoid arguing with each other. The teachers would make sure that never happened.

Solo was disappointed. He knew Mum played their piano every once in a while, and he quite liked that. But getting exposed to different instruments was a new experience for Solo. The guitar was great, but the flute? Well, Solo felt he couldn't get enough of that. So it was such a shame, then, that he couldn't hear it anymore. It simply made Solo want to sing.

The day of the concert drew closer and the entire family, including Solo, were getting more and more nervous about how the children would do. They had never played an instrument in front of an audience before. They even tried to talk their teachers into letting them not perform at all. But it was no use. They had to play.

The tension in the house was getting worse too, and every member of the family agreed, including Solo, that the sooner this concert was over the better. Even Solo's natural good temper was tested by the constant sniping between the siblings.

Finally, the day of the concert arrived. Even though it didn't seem possible, the tension the children were feeling was even worse. On the way to the concert, which was to be held in the school auditorium, the car was dead quiet. The children were thinking about what they had to do. The parents didn't want to say a word lest they upset the children in any way.

Solo, as usual, was in the back of the SUV. And, as usual, it had been debated whether Solo should even come along. But the children had insisted.

A friend of theirs at school was bringing her pet hamster as her lucky charm, and who could be more of a lucky dog than Solo? Mum and Dad where nervous about Solo being anywhere near the concert, but if Solo helped calm their children's nerves, well, then they were all for it.

The argument between Mum and Dad had not been about whether they should bring Solo; they had argued about who would be responsible for him. Dad had said Mum should hold Solo's lead as she was a calming influence on him. Mum had insisted that Dad should hold onto Solo as Solo was a very strong dog. Should he pull away, Dad was in a better position to hold on. This discussion only took place after the family got out of the car, and the children had said goodbye to their parents, but not before rubbing Solo's big, white head for luck.

In the end Mum, got her way. "Naturally," Dad thought as they followed the other parents into the auditorium.

At this point, they could have left Solo in the car, but once again, the children had insisted not only that Solo be present, but that they could see him from the stage. Dad had decided the best place for him was near the back, but in a position where his kids could see him and Solo.

Mum had wisely decided to go and sit with some other parents, well away from any mishaps Solo might cause. "Not that he would," she had said to Dad, "but you never know."

Dad didn't buy that argument for one second. He and Solo settled in at the back, Dad standing and Solo making himself comfortable by sitting on his haunches, a big grin on his face. Solo had never been to a concert before and was really looking forward to it. Especially as the youngest members of his human family would be performing.

Soon the lights dimmed and a group of children came on stage as part of a large brass band. They were *mostly* in tune and received warm applause when they had finished. Solo quite enjoyed the brass band; in particular he liked the trombone. That looked very interesting indeed.

Not for the first time, Solo wished his family would let him try more things. He made a mental note to see if you could borrow a trombone in the future.

Next up was the son. He had been given a solo spot just to play the acoustic guitar. He was that good.

Solo looked on proudly as the boy played a classical piece. Dad applauded loudly when his son had finished. He had no doubt his son's musical abilities came from his side of the family.

The rest of the acts were of various levels of skill. Some of the younger children sang as a choir and were so out of tune that Dad had to cover his face to try and suppress his laughter. Had his wife been near him, he no doubt would have heard all about his rude behavior on the ride home. And probably the next day too.

Solo, though, couldn't get enough of seeing the children singing their hearts out and playing their instruments. He hadn't really thought about it before, but decided he was now a lover of all things musical. If only he could join in somehow.

Finally it was the daughter's turn. She was part of a quartet that consisted of a violin, an oboe, a harp and the flute. They were the last act before the grand finale, when all the children would participate, with some singing and some playing their instruments.

Dad crossed his fingers as the quartet started to play. First a girl played oboe. She was soon joined by a boy on the violin. The music was beautiful. The entire audience was enchanted. Next was the harp, which added a haunting quality that echoed around the room. Finally, it was Solo's favorite member of the quartet to join in.

The daughter held her flute to her mouth, and ever so softly began to play. Once again, the entire audience was enchanted. This was the best act so far, they all thought.

Dad let out his breath, which he had been holding in due to the tension. "Okay," he thought, "we might actually get through this in one piece."

He spoke too soon.

Upon hearing the flute, Solo felt the urge to join in, just as he had weeks earlier when he was helping Dad grow those carrots. The flute was now getting louder and louder, leading the quartet through a stirring piece of music. Solo couldn't help it. He couldn't wait any longer and decided he wanted to join in. Right now. Right this very second.

Out of nowhere, piercing the room and echoing around and around, Solo started to howl in time to the music. Softly at first, like a low volume moan, but becoming louder and louder. Eventually ending up as a wolf howling at the moon. Only even louder and more piercing. At least a wolf howling at the moon was natural and to be expected. What was not to be expected was the sound of a large, white dog howling in the middle of a very delicate piece of music.

Dad, who had not been paying attention, had closed his eyes so as to savor the music coming from the stage, proud as could be that his daughter was doing such a good job. At first, he was as surprised as anyone when the howling started. "Where's that noise coming from?" he wondered. "How inconsiderate."

He looked around to see who was to blame. Then, with shock, he realized it was coming from the direction of his feet. He looked down, and there was Solo, howling at the top of his voice. Other parents around Dad gave him highly disapproving looks as the quartet on stage struggled to continue against the massive distraction coming from the back of the room.

Dad, finally understanding it was Solo making the noise as the entire audience turned to glare at him, attempted to pull Solo outside, but Solo was having none of it. He was singing along, he was enjoying the music, and he was not going anywhere.

In fact, taking Dad completely by surprise, he managed to pull the lead from Dad's grasp, run down the aisle, and jump on the stage. There he stood, right next to the daughter. The quartet would become a quintet if Solo had his way.

By now, though, the quartet had just about given up playing, but the daughter, who knew Solo only too well, kept going. The remaining quartet members gamely joined in to finish their piece with Solo howling at the top of his lungs alongside them.

Eventually they finished, and the entire audience stood to give them a standing ovation. Shouts of "bravo" and "encore" echoed throughout the auditorium. The quartet stood and bowed.

Solo beamed in satisfaction. "So this is what it feels like to be in front of an audience," he thought. "I must do this more often."

The grand finale took place as planned with all the children on stage, plus one extra; Solo was unanimously voted in to join them, howling along at the end at the top of his lungs. When the show was over and everyone filed out, they all agreed, this had been the best school concert ever.

16. Solo Goes Fishing

It was extremely early. The sun wasn't even up. It was rainy. The ground was soaked. And there was a heavy chill in the air. Normally this would be a perfect day for Dad to go golfing. But today was not a normal day for Dad. He had promised to go fishing with his friend.

"But you hate fishing," said Mum in surprise the night before.

"I know, I know," replied Dad, "but Steve was adamant that he needs moral support for the fishing competition. All I will do is fish a little and encourage him. What are friends for?"

As he got up from the warm bed and listened to the rain spatter against the windows, Dad was beginning to regret having friends like Steve. Now, if this early morning rise had been to play golf, he told himself, no problem. But fishing? All you did was sit on a small stool beside a cold river, probably shivering all day. Where's the fun in that? How does that compare to being on a windswept golf course, rain running down your neck, as you endeavor to get a tiny ball into a small hole? In Dad's eyes, there was no comparison.

As Dad sat at the large kitchen table, downed a large cup of hot black coffee, and poured the rest into a flask to keep it warm, he looked at Solo, who was in his usual spot under the table. Positioned not too close to the wood-burning stove to get too hot, but not too far away so he wouldn't get the benefit. It was, Solo had decided some time ago, quite the perfect spot.

"I am beginning to regret my offer, Solo," Dad said as peered under the table.

Solo raised his big head and looked at Dad. He had absolutely no idea what Dad was talking about, but whatever it was, Solo agreed. Dad sighed, drained the last of his coffee, pulled on his waterproof jacket, grabbed his seldom used fishing gear, and headed towards the backdoor. He looked down. Solo was waiting expectantly by his side.

"Solo," sighed Dad, "I'm sorry, boy, but you can't come."

Solo ignored Dad and continued to stare straight ahead at the unopened back door. Now, normally, if Dad was going to play golf in this weather at this unsavory hour, Solo would have been quite content to stay on his bed in the warm glow of the wood-burning stove. But today was different.

Dad was holding onto a strange looking long pole, which had what looked like a long, thin wire hanging from it, and a strange looking round thing at one end. Whatever it was that Dad was up to, Solo had decided that he wanted to be part of it. Whatever this long pole thingy was, Solo wanted to learn. This was something new. Solo was a very curious dog indeed.

Dad nudged Solo with his knee to prevent him from getting out as he opened the back door. But, as has been mentioned many times, Solo is a very persistent dog. He is also a very stubborn dog. Once his mind his made up, Solo tends to follow through. Of course, as is also known by now, he doesn't always plan very well, but we should at least admire his tenacity.

Dad's hands were full as he struggled to carry all the fishing gear, his basket of food and hot coffee, and open the door. This gave Solo the chance he needed, as Dad muttered under his breath once more about how he could be going to play golf instead. Then without thinking, he pressed the car remote to open the rear tailgate. Solo took his chance, and before Dad could stop him, Solo bolted past and jumped directly into the now open rear door of the car, where he waited expectantly for Dad.

"Solo!" yelled Dad. "Come back here now! I said you're not coming."

Solo continued to wait inside the cargo area of the SUV, looking around at the dark sky and the rain, as if he hadn't heard one word Dad had said. But, if Dad had paid attention, he would have noticed Solo was grinning from ear to ear.

But Dad wasn't paying attention. He was mad at himself for letting Solo get by him. And even more mad at himself for opening the rear door of the car without first making sure Solo was safely locked back in the house.

He reached the back of the car. "Solo, come on, boy. You're making me late. Let's go!" He slapped his thigh as best he could to emphasize that Solo needed to get out.

To make his point, Solo decided to lie down.

Dad let out an exasperated yell. Solo was the world's most stubborn dog, he thought. Although secretly, deep down, he was quite pleased that Solo was such an intelligent dog, and it was he, Dad, who had found him. Still, that didn't change the fact that Solo was where he shouldn't be. Yet again.

Dad tried once more. "Solo. Out. Now!"

Solo closed his eyes. Nap time before whatever this thing Dad was doing with that long pole began.

Just then, a trickle of water ran right down Dad's neck and down his spine. It was very cold. Dad thought for a second. He could either keep fighting with Solo and continue to stand in the rain, getting wetter and wetter, or he could just give up and let Solo come along. Dad decided that having Solo along would be okay after all. Besides, he would be company on what was undoubtedly going to be a long, wet, cold, and boring day.

Solo knew he'd won, although he really didn't think getting his way was actually winning. He knew that he could be great company for Dad on whatever this adventure was, and so in reality, he was doing Dad a favor by coming along instead of staying in the nice, warm kitchen on his nice, warm bed. Dad should appreciate the sacrifice Solo was making, thought Solo, who would be out with Dad on a cold, dark, and damp day.

Dad put his fishing gear in the car, closed the rear hatch, and off they went. As they drove down the narrow country lanes towards the river, the sun attempted to rise. But through the drizzle and the gray, it didn't seem to Dad that it was trying too hard.

Solo sat up, rested on his haunches, and looked around. He always enjoyed human watching, but on this gray, miserable day, most of the humans seemed to have agreed that the best thing to do was to stay in bed, pull the blankets over their heads, and grab some extra minutes of sleep.

As they approached the river, Dad could see a dozen or so cars parked along the bank with many of their owners already set up to fish. Their fishing lines had not been cast, as they all had to wait for the contest to begin. Some of the fishermen were chatting while drinking hot tea or coffee.

As Dad reversed back towards the river, his friend waved and came over to say hello. Dad parked and opened up the rear hatch of the SUV to get his fishing gear out, and then went to talk to his friend, who was waiting by the rear of the car.

Looking in and seeing Solo, Dad's friend leaned in and rubbed Solo's head. "I see you decided to bring Solo along," he said to Dad. "Good idea. You love a day out, don't you, Solo?"

Dad decided not to tell his friend he had tried to *stop* Solo from coming along.

As Dad had thoughtfully left the rear cargo door open, Solo could peer out into the consistent drizzle and watch what was happening without getting wet. This might not be so bad after all, thought Solo. "I get to stay dry, but I can see everything that's going on with this fishing thing."

Dad went down to the river to set up his fishing gear. After a few minutes, he returned and pulled out the flask of hot coffee, poured himself a cup, and sat down next to Solo at the back of the car. "See, Solo?" he said. "You can watch everything and see how well I do. Of course, you know I don't fish so I don't expect to do well. But you'll cheer me on. Won't you, boy?"

Seeing as Solo still had no idea what this fishing malarkey was about, Solo could only place his paw on Dad's knee to wish him luck. Solo wished any member of his family luck, even if he had absolutely no idea what it was they were about to do.

Dad had set his fishing line. Then, having checked in with the organizers and now wearing a number on his jacket, he waited along with everyone else for the go ahead to cast his line. At precisely eight o'clock, a soft whistle sounded, and all the anglers got to cast. Dad's friend did this extremely well. As did the other fisherman.

Dad, though, who was clearly out of practice, only succeeded in getting his line hooked into a nearby tree. A soft chuckle went up among the other fisherman. He tried again.

After a few more goes, he eventually managed to cast the line halfway into the river. Then, relieved he had at least done that, he sat down on his small foldout stool, and poured some more coffee. This is going to be a long morning, he thought, as another droplet of rain managed to find a way to dribble from his neck to his lower back. Dad shivered.

Solo watched all this with extreme interest. But, once all the lines were cast and the competitors were sitting down to watch their lines, Solo felt a giant sense of letdown. "Is that it?" he thought. "They simply throw a line into the river and wait? How is this any fun?" He decided that, perhaps, he had made a mistake after all in insisting he come along. He decided the best thing to do was to take a nap instead.

He had just closed his eyes when someone let out a yell. He sat up and looked down the riverbank. One of the competitors had caught a very large fish indeed. And only within a few minutes of the contest starting. A groan was let up from the other members of the competition, including Dad's friend. They all secretly prayed that the fish would be small.

It wasn't. The fish was quite large. It was weighed and measured before being put into large net that was submerged in the water to keep the fish safe until the competition was over. Then it would be released back into the river.

Solo found this extremely interesting. He now felt he understood fishing. You pulled a fish out of the river, then having looked at it, put it back again. At least to Solo this made more sense than golf, where all you did was try and hit a tiny ball into a tiny hole with a funny looking stick. Solo had once proven how easy golf was. He wondered if he could be good at fishing too.

He watched with interest for another half hour or so, but then, with nothing else exciting happening and the sound of the steady beat of rain on the roof of the car lulling him, he decided to take the nap he had put off earlier. But, as usual, he'd keep one ear open, just in case something exciting happened.

He had just done his usual circular routine before lying down to take his nap when some newcomers arrived. A girl with a fishing rod that was longer than she was tall, and what seemed to be her older brother. They set up their place on the river bank, only a few yards from Solo, on the other side of the SUV.

Solo watched with interest as the boy and girl attempted to get their lines into the river. Neither one succeeded. In the end, Dad, who was closest to the pair, came over to help them get their lines into the water.

With their lines only a few feet out from the bank of the river, the odds of the children catching anything was slim, but they certainly seemed to be having a grand old time regardless. Not for the first time, Solo marveled at how children could take something seemingly so simple and turn it into something very exciting indeed.

As Solo watched, the girl was wild in excitement, as if she expected fish to instantly jump onto her bait. Solo always hoped children would succeed, and when they didn't, he would often feel compelled to help. But in this case, amazingly, the little girl got a bite. Squealing in delight, she wound in her line. Solo stood up in the back of the SUV, barking encouragement.

The competitive fisherman frowned. "Who bought that noisy dog?" they thought. "We don't need that dog scaring the fish away."

Dad looked at his feet, secretly praying Solo would stop barking. Solo was praying too. In this case, hoping the girl would catch a big fish, but all the girl ended up catching was an old shoe which she threw back into the river in disgust.

She sat down on the wet river bank, folded her arms, and pouted. Her brother valiantly encouraged her to try again. Eventually, he got her line into the river, and she came over to hold the rod.

Meanwhile, at the competition where Dad and his friend were, other fisherman were having tremendous luck. One of Dad's friend's main rivals managed to reel in the largest catch of the day so far.

"Well, that's that," Dad's friend told him. "I don't imagine anyone for a second is going to catch a larger fish."

"Well, there's still time," said Dad encouragingly, who by now had started to enjoy fishing a little. It had one thing in common with golf, he decided. It was fun in the cold and the rain.

Solo continued to watch from the comfort of the back of the SUV until he realized that, in all the excitement of getting Dad to take him along, he'd forgotten to do his morning bathroom routine. Deciding he couldn't wait any longer, he jumped down from the back of the car in order to find a suitable spot to relieve himself.

As there weren't any suitable trees or bushes directly on the river bank, he went slightly downstream towards the girl and her brother. There he found a nice, large bush which he felt would be just right. Having relieved himself, Solo turned to walk back to the car. As he did so, he noticed the girl looking at him intently.

"Hello, boy," she said as he got closer.

Solo, always eager to make a new friend, went up to say hello.

The girl reached out to stroke his big, white head. "He's so soft," she told her brother.

Her brother wasn't paying any attention. He was too busy looking at the girl's fishing line. The float attached to it kept disappearing under the water.

"Look! Just look!" he said excitedly, as he pointed to the float which had popped up again. "Grab your rod, quickly," he shouted.

The girl, who had put her rod down in order to pet Solo, picked it up. Immediately, the line tightened, and the float disappeared completely. "I've caught something. I've caught something!" she yelled at the top of her lungs. She was so loud even the competitors from just up the river turned to look.

She started winding in the catch, but it was too heavy. So she decided it would be easier to simply pull the catch up by holding the rod, and walking backwards up the bank. Solo watched in amazement as the girl tried to pull the catch in, but it was no good; it was simply too heavy. Her brother came over to help. He was just about to grab the rod also when the giant fish pulled back.

Taken by surprise, the rod, the line, and the girl, were thrown into the water, she was so shocked that she wouldn't let go of the rod. Now screaming for help, her brother watched helplessly as she was pulled towards the middle of the river. Several of the adults further up the river saw what was happening and rushed to help. But Solo beat them to it.

Without even thinking, he jumped in the icy river and swam after the girl, who by now had been carried downstream at an ever-increasing rate. Solo was a young, strong dog, but even he had to stretch himself in order to catch up to the girl. Swimming as fast and as hard as he could, he was able to reach the girl, who amazingly was still holding onto her fishing rod. As scared as she was, she wasn't about to let her catch get away.

About a hundred yards from where she had fallen in, Solo was able to grab hold of the girls collar in his mouth. Normally Solo could easily have swam to shore with her, but she was wearing heavy clothing and still hanging onto the poll. It was all Solo could do to prevent them both from being swept further downstream.

Slowly but surely, Solo was able to steer the girl, her rod, and the fish towards the side of the river. As they got closer, several fishermen jumped into the water to help get them out. As they grabbed the girl, she lost hold of her rod, and the fish was able to pull it back towards the middle of the river. She screamed in despair.

Solo, who was being helped out by Dad and his friend, noticed the girls yelling, and ignoring Dad's call to, "Come back, Solo!" swam after the rod, which was floating on the top of the water, being pulled along by the fish at a high rate of speed.

Reaching the rod, he grabbed the handle in his large mouth, and swimming once more to the side of the river, pulled it onto shore. The girl, her brother, Dad, his friend, and the entire group of fishermen watched as Solo pulled up not only the rod and the fishing line, but the largest fish he'd ever seen.

As an exhausted Solo lay down on the bank in order to catch his breath, the girl ran over and gave him one of the biggest hugs he had ever received. Then one of the fishermen grabbed the fishing line and held up the fish. It was so large, he needed both hands to hold the struggling fish.

That night, an exhausted Solo slept soundly as Dad explained to his amazed family what Solo had done. Everyone from the fishing tournament had decided the girl and Solo deserved first place in the fishing competition, even though they weren't even entered.

It was no surprise to the family then, that the next day when their local newspaper was delivered, that Solo was yet again photographed on the cover, with the large fish and the girl next to him on the river bank, and the headline, "Fisherman Solo."

"Typical," said Dad. "Solo wasn't even in the competition, but he still won."

"You should be very proud, dear," said his wife. "After all, as you constantly remind us, you're the one who found Solo."

"Well there is that," said Dad, proudly.

17. Solo and the Old Man

Solo and his family were walking down the street in the busy town close to where they lived. It was a chilly day, with people bundled up against a brisk, north wind. They had scarves around their necks and, if they had one, they pulled their hoods over their heads.

Mum and Dad had decided to come into town as they were in desperate need of a few household essentials that were not sold in their small, village store. Dad had tried to get out of coming, as he felt that having both parents come on such a simple mission was a waste of time, but Mum had insisted. What Dad really wanted to do was play golf.

Dad would play golf in any weathers if he could. Once, he had played golf during a raging blizzard. The only reason he had to stop was when he started to lose too many golf balls in the large snow drifts. So for him to play during a cold and blustery day like today would be very easy indeed.

Somewhat grumpily therefore, he had agreed to come along. And if Mum and Dad *and* the children were going, then Solo was going too. He made sure of this by running out the front door the moment it was opened, then placing himself strategically at the rear hatch of the family SUV, and refusing to move unless they opened the hatch to let him jump in.

On a cold day like this, Solo could be safely left in the car, and normally he would have been quite content just to sit there and people watch. And wonder, as he often did, when humans scurried here and there, "What is it that humans find to do all the time? Why can't they just relax?"

But today, Solo was in such a rush to jump into the back of the car, that he forget to go the bathroom first. This meant by the time they had parked the car, Solo was in desperate need to go number one. Recognizing Solo's anxious look, Dad let Solo out. He promptly jumped down, and relieved himself on the wheel of a very expensive looking car parked nearby. Unfortunately, Solo chose to do this just as the extremely well-dressed lady owner of the car showed up.

She looked down at the large puddle next to her wheel. Then she looked at Solo, who quite wisely refused to look at her. Finally, her gaze turned to Dad. She gave him a withering look.

All Dad could mutter was, "Sorry," and he dragged Solo back to the open rear of the SUV.

Solo looked at the rear door and decided he was not getting in. He was out now, so he might as well come along. No amount of coaching by his family could get Solo to jump into the back of the car, so somewhat reluctantly, they decided to bring him along.

"Don't blame me if he does something," said Dad to his wife.

"The walk will do him good, dear," she replied. "And we won't have to take him for a walk later. It's supposed to get even colder."

Dad, following Mum's logic, decided she was right. Still, just to be safe, he held on to Solo's lead very tightly indeed.

The first stop was the hardware store, where Dad needed to pick up some new tools. It was decided that bringing Solo into a store with nails, hammers, drills, saws and much more was far too risky. So Solo stayed outside with Mum. After what seemed like an eternity, Dad came out. His wife, now half-frozen, reminded Dad that next time she spent a long time trying on a dress, he'd better think twice before complaining.

The next stop was the bank. A place where Solo could not really do any harm. With the weather starting to get colder, no one was interested in waiting outside with Solo anyway. Solo of course didn't mind the weather. He had a lovely fur coat to keep him warm.

Solo liked the cold too. He could quite happily play outside all day even when it was snowing. In particular when it was snowing. Snow was one of Solo's favorite things. That and ice cream, naps, tennis balls, and his family.

As the family entered the bank, Dad let out a groan. "Just look at all these people." And sure enough, the bank was very busy with people waiting to take care of business. Dad motioned his family to sit down on some chairs that were placed around the bank. "This might take some time," he told them, "or you can go and get some coffee and I'll meet you."

Given the choice between waiting in a crowded, stuffy bank or a nice, cozy coffee shop, Mum and the kids chose the coffee shop. Solo, though, was fascinated by the bank. He had no idea what a bank was, but he thought it must be very important indeed as all these people were waiting for something. He had been to the coffee shop many times, and while it was true the owners tended to make a fuss over him and put down a bowl of water, he was never actually allowed to have coffee. Solo couldn't see the point of going to a shop that specialized in coffee if he, Solo, wasn't allowed to drink any.

Solo made his point known by nuzzling Dad's leg and standing right beside him as they waited to be served behind about six people.

"I think Solo wants to stay with you, Dad," said his son.

"No way," said Dad. "I've business to conduct." But before he could do anything, his family abandoned him to take care of Solo.

Mum waived as she left, giving Dad a smile that said, "Have fun."

"Just us boys, huh, Solo?" he said to Solo. Dad made sure to keep a tight hold of Solo's lead. Even in something as boring and uninteresting as a bank, Dad didn't trust Solo not to get up to any mischief.

Solo, meanwhile, was exponentially pleased with himself. He had succeeded in not going to the boring coffee shop. Instead, he now got to learn what a bank was.

He looked around as they waited. People, all dressed in their warm weather gear, seemed to be waiting to speak to people who, for some reason, sat behind windows. Why there were windows inside the building made no sense to Solo. Although, he was sure he would find out soon enough.

The people behind the glass must be very important indeed, thought Solo, as those on the side of the glass where Dad and Solo were all seemed to be asking the important people for something. Some were even waving their arms around and demanding to "speak to the manager", whoever that was.

Slowly, they got closer to the important people behind the glass. As they waited, Solo had plenty of time to look at the other people who were also waiting. But one in particular caught Solo's attention.

It was an old man, pulling a beaten up, four-wheeled, red, child's wagon. Sitting in the wagon was a little, white dog. Despite the fact the old man looked quite poor, what with his dirty, old, plastic raincoat and even dirtier flat cap, the dog looked clean and well cared for. The dog was sitting on an old towel, and to complete the look, there was a homemade plastic cover protecting half of the wagon from the elements.

The old man's rain coat hung loosely around his bent and rounded shoulders. The raincoat's belt was missing, and it was torn in a couple of places. His shoes seemed old and worn, yet somehow comfortable. They were so old that they appeared to be an extension of the man's feet. The whole effect seemed to be one of a man who had seen too many years of hard times, and Solo sensed he was about to give up.

The old man, the wagon, and the dog were only a few feet away from Solo and Dad. Solo moved closer to the small dog without pulling too hard on his lead. Dad was not really paying attention anyway as he was talking to an old friend he had bumped into at the bank.

Solo went up to the small dog and gave him a good sniff. He certainly smelled healthy, thought Solo. The little dog stood up on his wagon, wagged his tail, and licked Solo's nose.

Just then, the old man noticed Solo, knelt down, and rubbed his big head. "Well, you're a fine lookin' fella, I must say," he said to Solo.

Solo sniffed the old man. Grateful as he was for the head rub, Solo noticed the old man definitely did not smell as nice as the little dog. Still, as Solo had been known to sniff some quite disgusting things when going for walks, the old man's smell was not quite as off-putting to Solo as it was to the old man's fellow humans.

Just then, the old man was called to the counter by one of the very important people behind the glass. He pulled the wagon and the dog along with him. Solo wanted to go too, but Dad kept a firm grip on Solo's lead.

Solo pulled harder. Dad gripped harder. Solo pulled harder still. Dad held Solo's lead harder still. But Dad, noticing all Solo wanted to do was see the small dog, and tiring of holding onto Solo's lead, decided to let go so he could focus on talking to his friend, who was in the middle of telling a very funny story.

Free to wander a little, Solo walked over to the old man and the dog, who was still sitting comfortably in his little, red wagon. Once again, Solo and the dog rubbed noses and sniffed. Both dogs wagged their tails vigorously. Above him, talking to a very important person behind the glass, Solo could hear what the old man was saying.

"But there is enough money in the account. I know there is. If I can't pay my electric bill soon, they will cut it off."

"I'm sorry sir," said the lady behind the glass. "You don't have any money in your account. In fact,"—she lowered her voice, but Solo could still hear—"you are overdrawn, sir." And she wrote down something on a small piece of paper and handed it to the old man.

The old man let out a sigh and lowered his head, as if he knew he was fighting a lost cause.

Solo, who had taken an immediate liking to the old man even if he didn't smell particularly nice, decided to see if he could help. Noticing that Dad had his back to him, he jumped up, placing his front paws on the counter, and stuck his big head directly into the glass, giving what he knew was his best "Hi, I'm Solo" smile.

The lady behind the glass was taken aback. "Good gracious," she said, "That took me by surprise."

"Me too," said the old man, glancing down at Solo. "Where did you come from?" The old man liked Solo, but he had bigger problems to deal with right now. "Get down. There's a good lad," he said.

But Solo simply ignored him, and instead continued to stare his "Hi, I'm Solo" face at the lady. Solo was an obedient dog, unless he was told to do something he didn't want to do. And Solo didn't want to get down. He felt his mere presence could help remedy the situation, but even Solo couldn't conjure up money into the old man's bank account out of nowhere.

The old man turned back to the lady. "I just need a small amount to tide me over until my pension comes in. Can I speak to the manager?"

The lady looked at him, then at Solo who was still smiling at her, his big dark eyes attempting to work their magic. Still looking directly at Solo, she said, "Sir, I don't think it will help, but if you give me one minute, I will get him for you." She sighed, got off her stool and disappeared into the back of the bank.

The old man leaned down and whispered to Solo, "Keep your fingers crossed, lad. Or toes, I suppose. Perhaps you'll bring me some luck, huh, boy?"

Solo agreed, but the man's breath was as bad as the rest of his smell. Solo decided, and not for the first time, that while Solo never needed a bath, humans certainly did.

Just then, Dad turned around and noticed Solo resting his front paws on the counter right next to the old man. "I'm sorry," he said to the man as he walked over. "Is my dog bothering you? "

"Not at all," said the old man. "In fact, he's a keeping me company."

Dad was about to insist that Solo get down when he was called to the counter by another very important person behind the glass. Seeing that the old man was a harmless eccentric, he left Solo where he was for a few minutes.

Solo was pleased. He liked to make new friends, even if they did smell a bit, but he really wanted to learn what banks were all about. So far, he couldn't make heads or tails about what purpose they served.

Solo and the old man didn't have long to wait before the lady returned, bringing with her a short, balding, and somewhat sweaty man. She introduced him as the manager of the bank. Solo took an immediate dislike to him. Solo usually liked everybody unless they gave him a reason not to, but he always gave people the benefit of the doubt. For some reason Solo felt this little man was the cause of the old man's problems. Solo decided to fix him with one of his icy stares.

Solo's ability to stare at someone without blinking was legend amongst his family. If he wanted to make a point, or if he wanted something, Solo had the ability, it seemed, to remain fixed in one position, never wavering, for hours on end. Most people gave up trying to compete with Solo after only a few minutes. It certainly made all recipients of Solo's stare uncomfortable.

The bank manager leaned into the glass and spoke to the old man. "I'm very sorry," he said, "but I know it's been explained to you. You already have an overdraft which I can't extend, and..." Just then, he looked down and caught sight of Solo for the first time. Immediately, he felt drawn into Solo's gaze. He tried again. "I'm sorry, Mr. huh, Mr. huh." He stopped again, once more feeling the pull of Solo.

He felt the sweat start to bead on his forehead. What was it about this is dog? He attempted another go. "Sir, as has been explained to you, the bank..." His voice trailed off a third time. *Get a grip*, he told himself.

What he really wanted to do was to get back to his cozy office and continue the crossword puzzle, not deal with some smelly, old man and his clearly manic dog. Realizing he'd lost his way, he tried again. "Um...er," was all he could mutter.

The woman standing next to him leaned over and whispered, "Are you having a stroke? What's wrong with you?"

The bald man looked directly into Solo's eyes, which was a mistake. He felt as if Solo had some kind of mind control over him. *That darn dog hasn't moved or blinked once since I got here*, he thought. Deciding retreat was best, and knowing a cup of tea would do him well, he told the lady to expand the old man's overdraft after all.

With a surprised look, she then handed out some cash to the old man as the bank manager went back to his office, closed the door, and slumped into his big office chair. He pulled out a large white handkerchief and wiped his forehead, wishing as he did so, that he would never have to see that dog again.

Back inside the bank, Solo jumped down from the counter and once again on all fours, walked over to Dad who had just finished his business. "I trust Solo was no bother," said Dad. "He's a very inquisitive dog."

The old man stroked Solo's head. "Oh no. He was great help." He waved his money in front of Dad.

"He was?" said Dad. "How?"

But the old man was already out the door, pulling his little, red wagon and little, white dog behind him.

As Dad led Solo out into the rainy street and towards the coffee shop where they were to meet the rest of the family, Dad watched for the old man, but he seemed to have disappeared. Looking up and down the street, Dad couldn't see him. "That's weird," said Dad to himself. As they kept walking, Dad looked down at Solo, and wondered not for the first time, *What is it about Solo anyway?*

The Real Solo

Many of the adventures in this book are fictional, but the lazy, excitable, friendly, mischievous, overly hairy, big, beautiful shelter dog described is very real. Solo continues to inspire more fantastic tales, and we hope you'll be back for them.

About the Author

The story of how Dad found Solo at the Dog Rescue is based upon how the author found the real Solo. He was a new arrival and kenneled in an area marked, "No Admittance", which, just like Dad, the author ignored. This inspired Jonathan Langley to write the Solo stories.

Jonathan Langley is a native of the UK.

About the Illustrator

In 2014, Stefanie Schultz graduated the University of Texas at Austin with a dual major in Studio Art and English Literature. She was always passionate about the relationship between art and fiction. She found that her favorite novels stimulated her imagination and inspired her to create some of her best artwork. After graduation Stefanie began her career as a medical illustrator but continued her love for reading and drawing in her free time.

The Adventures of Solo is Stefanie's first illustrated book.

Made in the USA
Columbia, SC
08 October 2021

46519163R00157